126708

KT-393-761

Daniel could almost feel months of scheming crashing around his ears

Not to mention that his life was pretty much flashing in front of his eyes. One significant memory from his past had apparently materialised and was now sitting right next to him on Judson Drake's private jet.

She looked pale, he noted. And no wonder. Her head was probably spinning.

He knew his was.

He had thought himself prepared for any eventuality on this trip. He had not been at all prepared for Brittany Jeanne Samples to walk through that door—and directly into his arms.

Available in November 2006
from Silhouette Special Edition

The Borrowed Ring

GINA WILKINS

SILHOUETTE®

SPECIAL EDITION™

Silhouette, Silhouette Special Edition and Colophon are registered trademarks of Harlequin Books S.A., used under licence.

First published in Great Britain 2006
Silhouette Books, Eton House, 18-24 Paradise Road,
Richmond, Surrey TW9 1SR

© Gina Wilkins 2005

ISBN-13: 978 0 373 24717 2
ISBN-10:0 373 24717 6

23-1106

Printed and bound in Spain
by Litografia Rosés S.A., Barcelona

GINA WILKINS

is a bestselling and award-winning author who has written more than seventy books. She credits her successful career in romance to her long, happy marriage and her three "extraordinary" children.

A lifelong resident of central Arkansas, Ms Wilkins sold her first book to Harlequin in 1987 and has been writing full-time since. She has appeared on the Waldenbooks and *USA TODAY* bestseller lists. She is a three-time recipient of the Maggie Award for Excellence, sponsored by Georgia Romance Writers, and has won several awards from the reviewers of *Romantic Times*.

Chapter One

B.J. Samples. Private investigator extraordinaire.

Almost strutting with pride, she climbed out of her rental car and approached the Missouri farmhouse that lay at the end of a long, wide driveway. Actually *farmhouse* did not do the structure justice. This was practically a mansion. Pillars, dormers, balconies. Fountains and a swimming pool and detached pool house. Landscaping that looked like a photograph from a home-and-garden magazine. There was even a private airstrip behind the house.

Having come from a childhood of poverty and homelessness, Daniel Castillo—now known as Daniel Andreas—had apparently done quite well for himself.

He had not, however, been an easy man to find. She had spent the past week trying to track him down, finally getting a lead that had brought her to this spreading east Missouri farm an hour's drive from St. Louis. It hadn't been effortless, but she had gotten the information. And she couldn't wait to boast about it to her three uncles who owned the private investigation agency that employed her.

Her confident steps slowed as she approached the front door. She had the oddest feeling that she was being watched. She glanced around and saw no one, not even in the many highly polished windows at the front of the house.

Maybe it was just an attack of nerves. After all, she didn't usually do fieldwork. Computer searches were her specialty. The only reason she had been sent on this trip was because it was a low-priority assignment. One that could hardly get her into any trouble.

Maybe it was the place itself that was getting to her. Her hand wasn't quite steady when she reached for the doorbell. Was it any wonder? The only mansion she had ever visited regularly in her middle-class upbringing was her wealthy aunt Michelle's. Yet with Tony and Michelle's four children and assortment of pets, that sprawling estate had always been homey and welcoming.

She glanced down at her olive-green camp shirt and khaki pants. Perhaps she should have dressed more professionally. But it was too late for that now. The front door opened, and a very large, very bald man in a shiny gray jacket, a pale blue shirt and sharply creased jeans growled, "Yes?"

He didn't look like a butler. Nor a farmer, for that matter. He looked more like a bouncer in a low-rent strip joint. Not that she'd ever actually been in a place like that. Drawing herself to her full five feet three inches—still a foot shorter than this man—B.J. tried to speak confidently. "I'm looking for Daniel Andreas. Is he here?"

The man's heavy eyebrows rose toward his shaved pate. "Daniel Andreas?"

Never known as a particularly patient woman, B.J. swallowed a sigh. "That's what I said."

Comprehension seemed to light in his dull brown eyes. "Oh! You made it. I'm sure he'll be pleased. Come in."

She didn't have a clue what he was talking about. "I don't—"

"Daniel!" the man bellowed, practically hauling her inside. He glanced toward the staircase. "Oh, there you are. Look who's here. Your missus."

B.J. glanced in the same direction, then simply stared. She had wondered how Daniel would look in person after thirteen years. Now she knew.

He looked fantastic.

For a moment he stared back at her, no expression at all on his incredibly handsome face. She doubted sincerely that he recognized her. It had been too long, and she was sure she had not made the impression on him back then that he had on her.

Before she could speak, he was coming toward her with swift, graceful movements that were vaguely feline. Just a bit predatory. The smile that lit his face was blinding, but she had a moment to notice that his obsidian eyes were deadly serious before he grabbed her and yanked her toward him. "Darling! I'm so glad you could make it after all."

A moment later his mouth was on hers in a kiss hot enough to melt the soles of her leather sandals.

When the kiss ended, he didn't give her a chance to speak—even if she had been able to, which certainly wasn't guaranteed just then. Gripping her shoulders hard enough to leave fingerprints, he looked at the bald man, who hovered nearby with an oddly sentimental smile on his broad face. "Bernard, would you give us a minute alone? We have some catching up to do."

Bernard? B.J. found herself mentally repeating. Was that really that man's name?

The big man nodded. "You and the missus can use that little parlor just behind you. You won't be disturbed. I'll let you know when we have to go. In the meantime, I'll call the boss and tell him your wife will be joining us, after all."

"Oh, but—"

Daniel's fingers dug more sharply into B.J.'s shoulders, causing her words to end in a gasp. "Yes, do that," he said to the other man.

Bernard was frowning at B.J. "Something wrong, Mrs. Andreas?"

She glanced up at Daniel in bewilderment. The look

he gave her in return had her turning back to Bernard with a strained smile. "I just need to talk to my, er, to Daniel in private for a moment."

The large man's face cleared, his somewhat scary-looking smile returning. "Right this way, ma'am."

He ushered them into an elegantly furnished little parlor and closed the door behind him to leave them alone.

B.J. whirled immediately to face Daniel, making no effort now to hide her outrage. "What the hell was that?"

"Please keep your voice down." He had dropped the smile, and his face was an expressionless mask again as he studied her. "You have no idea how you've complicated everything."

Her jaw almost dropped. *She* had complicated everything? Had she just walked into an expensive mad-house?

Because she needed a moment to collect herself or she would end up shrieking at him, she studied the man who stood in front of her, comparing him to the boy she had once briefly known. He had fascinated her when she was fourteen and he was sixteen. Even then he had been striking looking, with his thick black hair, classic features and lazy-lidded dark eyes.

Some of her cousins had been a little afraid of his flash-point temper, but B.J. never had been. There had been something about him that had drawn her into girl-ish daydreams and amorous fantasies. He had been her first big crush, and she had never forgotten him.

Now he was a man of almost thirty. Still handsome

but seemingly more comfortable in his skin now. The jeans, T-shirt and boots of his youth had been traded for a dark jacket that must have cost a small fortune, worn over an open-necked white shirt, charcoal slacks and expensive-looking shoes.

He looked rich, powerful and more than just a little dangerous. Still, she refused to let him see that she was at all intimidated.

Lifting her chin, she placed her hands on her slim hips and spoke firmly. "Obviously there has been some mistake. I don't know who you and Bernard were expecting, but you have the wrong person. My name is—"

"Brittany Samples," he cut in coolly. "I recognized you as soon as you walked in."

For the second time since she arrived, he had rendered her speechless. How on earth had he identified her that quickly? It had been more than a dozen years, for crying out loud. The last time he had seen her, she had been a shy fourteen-year-old with braces and no figure at all.

Well, okay, she still didn't have much of a figure. She had long ago given up on naturally growing big breasts or voluptuous hips. But still, she was a grown woman of twenty-seven now. She wore her brown hair layered in a choppy short cut that she'd been told was flattering to her lamentably gamine face and she had applied her makeup in a way that played up her blue eyes.

The fact that she had recognized *him* so easily didn't lessen her surprise. After all, she had been expecting to find him. She had a fairly recent snapshot of him in her wallet. And she had carried a mental picture at the back of her mind for years. She doubted he could say the same about her.

Finally recovering, she stammered slightly when she said, "I, um, really didn't expect you to know me. How did you—"

He made a silencing movement with his right hand. "We don't have time for this now. We've got to figure out how to get you out of this mess you've created without putting either of us in any more danger."

"The mess *I've* created?" she repeated incredulously. And then the rest of his words registered. "Danger?"

Daniel put a hand to the back of his neck and squeezed, his brow creased in concentration. "Maybe we should tell them…"

"The truth?" she suggested when his words faded.

"That's not going to work."

"Look—" She took a step toward him, bringing her close enough to jab a finger of her left hand into his chest. "I don't know what's going on here, but I've had enough. All I came here to do was—"

He caught her hand in his, absently pulling it away from his chest but not releasing her. "Bernard thinks you're my wife. If he has any reason to suspect either of us is not who we've said, he'll kill us. And, by the way, he's not the only armed guard surrounding us. The house is crawling with them—and every one of them answers to him."

She felt her stomach clench. "I don't believe you."

"Believe it, Brittany."

Focusing on that name rather than the fear that was suddenly trying to overtake her, she scowled. "I answer to B.J. Any husband worth his salt would know that."

Ignoring her heavily sarcastic remark, he continued, "We don't have much time, so you must listen. How did you get here?"

"I drove from St. Louis. Why?"

"Your own car or a rental?"

"A rental. I don't—"

He seemed to be concentrating on his own thoughts rather than her attempts to turn the questioning back on him. "Do you have any luggage with you?"

"No, I left it all at my hotel. Daniel—"

He studied her left hand, which he still held. "No rings. Not married?"

"No." She couldn't help noticing the gold band on his left hand. "So where is your real wife?"

"I'll explain later." Reaching inside the collar of his white shirt, he fished out a thin gold chain, which he swiftly unfastened. A moment later he had her left hand in his again. His eyes locked with hers as he slid a ring onto her finger.

Dazed, she looked down at the simple, aged-looking gold ring. "This is a wedding ring," she said stupidly.

A sharp rap on the door barely gave warning of Bernard's abrupt entrance. He caught them still standing close together, seemingly holding hands. "Sorry to interrupt the reunion, but we really have to get under way."

"There has been a problem, Bernard. My wife was just telling me she can't join us." Daniel's voice held a touch of regret as he slipped an arm around her shoulders.

Bernard's heavy face settled into a frown. "What's the problem?"

"Her luggage has been misplaced by the airline. The only garments she has with her are the ones she's wearing." He spoke so smoothly B.J. almost believed him herself.

Bernard scanned her casual camp shirt and khakis, nodding as if something had just been explained to him. "That's not a problem. You can buy everything she needs when we get there. We've got several of those fancy boutiques the ladies like."

After only a momentary pause, Daniel said, "She has some things in her luggage that have sentimental value. She's reluctant to leave without tracking it down."

His frown deepening, Bernard shifted restlessly. Suspiciously. The movement made his ill-fitting jacket gap just enough for B.J. to catch a glimpse of the shoulder holster beneath. "I'm sure the boss can take care of everything. Why don't we get going and I'll make some calls on the way."

B.J. thought she detected the slightest hint of apology in the look Daniel gave her then. "There's really no need to go to that much trouble. You have our home address on your luggage tags, don't you, sweetheart?"

Remembering the chilling sight of Bernard's weapon, B.J. nodded mutely.

"Then I'm sure it will all be sent to our home as soon as it turns up. In any event, there's really nothing all that valuable involved, is there?"

She shook her head, as he clearly expected of her.

Daniel gave her an encouraging smile.

Bernard's face cleared. "That's okay, then. You'll see, Mrs. Andreas. Everything's going to work out just fine."

She wished she could believe that.

Daniel could almost feel months of scheming crashing around his ears. Not to mention that his life was pretty much flashing in front of his eyes. One significant memory from his past had apparently materialized and was now sitting right next to him on Judson Drake's private jet.

She looked pale, he noted. And no wonder. Her head was probably spinning.

He knew his was.

He had thought himself prepared for any eventuality on this trip. He had not been at all prepared for Brittany Jeanne Samples to walk through that door—and directly into his arms.

She hadn't really changed in thirteen years, he mused. Oh, there were definitely signs of maturity. She had worn braces the last time he'd seen her. Now her white teeth were perfectly straight. Her glossy brown hair had fallen almost to her waist back then, and it was now cut into a short, shaggy style that suited her.

Her figure hadn't developed significantly since her

teenage years, but rather than the gawkiness of adolescence, she now moved with the lithe grace of womanhood. And her eyes were still an amazingly rich blue, still framed in ridiculously long, lush lashes.

Some might call her cute or even pretty. However one defined it, her look appealed to him as strongly now as it had when he was sixteen.

He had never expected to see her again—certainly not under these conditions. He hadn't had a chance yet to analyze how he felt about having her here, other than fear for her safety and concern about the plans he had spent so long putting together. Still, at the back of his mind was the uncomfortable awareness that Brittany Jeanne Samples was the only living soul who had ever seen him cry.

Thirteen years ago, she was the only one he knew, other than his foster parents, who hadn't been at all afraid of him. She wasn't afraid now. Quietly furious, yes. Healthily cautious, definitely. But not afraid.

Yet he reached out to pat her hand, giving her a bracing smile. "I know how much you hate flying in these small planes. Are you okay?"

"I'm fine."

"Don't you worry, Mrs. Andreas," Bernard said with a heavy-handed attempt at sympathy. "Mr. Drake hires only the best pilots."

Her strained expression didn't change. "I'm sure he does."

"Can I get you anything? Soda? Bottled water?"

"No, thank you."

Daniel trusted that Bernard would attribute B.J.'s terseness to a fear of flying, as he had intended when he had mentioned it. Bernard wasn't the sharpest pencil in the cup, but he wasn't entirely unobservant either. B.J. was hardly acting like a loving wife on her way to a luxurious resort with her husband.

He was going to have to be on his toes every minute to cover for her. He really hadn't needed this complication.

They were in the air for almost four hours. While Bernard played a video game built into a console in the private jet and Daniel read what appeared to be a book about the Spanish-American War, B.J. simply stared out a side window.

She declined the magazines Bernard offered her and had no interest in watching the television he pointed out to her. She was unable to doze. She spent the time wondering where they were going and why and what to expect when they got there.

Had she made a huge mistake going along with this charade? Should she have made it clear that she was not Daniel's wife? Perhaps treated it as a joke? But he had given her little time for that option and he had looked deadly serious when he'd told her that her very life was in danger.

Seeing the gun tucked beneath Bernard's jacket had seemed to illustrate that warning quite clearly.

Still, was she any safer now, flying toward who knew where for who knew what purpose?

Daniel spoke to her occasionally, using a lovingly solicitous tone that made her back teeth set. She had to make a real effort to respond in kind, but apparently her acting skills were better than she had thought, since Bernard didn't seem to notice anything unusual between them. Maybe because Daniel mentioned several times her supposed fear of flying and commented about how brave she was being, even though he knew she must be anxious.

She hadn't been afraid of flying, but this nightmare trip could definitely leave permanent trauma, she decided.

When they finally landed, it was on another private airstrip. From what B.J. could guess from peering out the window, this strip was a part of a luxurious oceanside resort. She had seen swimming pools and cabanas, sprawling buildings and cozy cabins. Private beaches. Two golf courses.

Florida? South Carolina? She really had no clue.

Maybe the place would have looked more beautiful to her had she been arriving for a voluntary stay. As it was, the only thought on her mind was wondering how soon she could leave.

"See, Mrs. Andreas?" Bernard asked jovially. "Back on the ground, safe and sound."

She would have liked very much to smack him right in the middle of his condescending smile. Instead she merely nodded.

Once again Daniel spoke for her. "My wife is exhausted from so much traveling today. I hope we can be shown to our suite quickly so she can get some rest."

B.J. hoped that suite had a back door she could dash out of as soon as no one was looking. At the very least, she would be on the phone at the first opportunity telling her uncles to get busy rescuing her. Well, she would make that call as soon as she figured out where she was.

Bernard ushered them off the plane. A man stepped forward immediately to greet them. In marked contrast to the beefy and belligerent-looking Bernard, this man was handsome, slender and suave. Yet something about his smile made B.J.'s blood run cold.

His heavily moussed hair was sun-streaked blond, and his eyes were a glittering green. He had a perfect profile, a perfect tan, perfect teeth and a perfect physique. She would have bet hard-earned cash that none of those attributes had been bestowed upon him by nature.

As her cowboy uncle Jared would say, this fellow was so slick she could have slid him through a keyhole.

"Daniel," he said, shaking Daniel's hand. "It's good to see you again. And this—" he turned to B.J. "—must be your lovely wife."

His voice practically coated with pride, Daniel replied, "Yes, this is B.J. Darling, I'd like you to meet Judson Drake, the man I've told you so much about."

Judson Drake. If that was his real name, she would eat her shoe.

She nearly flinched when Drake took her hand, holding it more snugly than necessary. "It's my pleasure to meet you, Mrs. Andreas."

"Mr. Drake," she murmured. As much as it unnerved

her to be called Mrs. Andreas, she didn't encourage him to use her nickname.

"Bernard tells me that you've had a difficult time. I understand that your luggage has been misplaced."

He was still holding her hand. B.J. gave a slight tug, freeing it, before she replied, "Yes. I suggested that I should stay behind…"

"Nonsense." He waved a hand dismissively. "We have everything you could need in our shops here. I'll make arrangements for you to select whatever you like. Just give the shopkeepers your name, and anything you need is yours."

"That's very generous of you, but I can provide for my wife's needs," Daniel said with a hint of bruised pride. "If you'll make arrangements for her to charge her purchases to our suite, that will be sufficient."

Drake eyed Daniel with a speculation B.J. couldn't quite analyze. "Consider it done. I'm sure you're both tired and hungry. Perhaps you would like to take advantage of some of my resort's amenities for the remainder of the day. We can talk business tomorrow, Daniel."

Daniel seemed to give the suggestion some thought, and then he inclined his head. "Thank you. For my wife's sake, I think that would be best."

If he said "my wife" in that smugly possessive tone one more time, B.J. was going to kick him. Hard. And she didn't care who was watching.

"Let me escort you to your suite. Bernard will see that your bags are delivered to you, Daniel."

Tucking her canvas tote bag beneath her arm—and

thinking wistfully of the cell phone tucked inside it—
B.J. allowed herself to be led to the main lodge of the
resort. They passed other people, mostly wealthy-look-
ing and highly maintained couples, but other than smiling genially, Drake did not allow himself to be detained.

He led them through an exquisitely decorated lobby,
merely nodding to the young woman behind the recep-
tion desk. He kept up a congenial-host monologue during a brief elevator ride, listing some of the resort's
many attractions.

Drake stood much closer to B.J. than she thought
necessary; the elevator car was not so small that it re-
quired that proximity. When he escorted them into a
luxurious suite, his hand rested casually at the small of
her back, just above the very slight curve of her hip.

Drake was so vainly assured of his appeal to women
that he seemed to expect her to fall at his feet—even
with her "husband" standing right next to them. She
wondered how he would react if she informed him that
his touch made her want to scrub her skin with bleach.

Telling them he was leaving them to relax, he made
a swift exit, pausing only long enough to remind Daniel that they would schedule a meeting for the next
morning.

The moment the door closed behind him, B.J.
whirled to face Daniel. "If that man touches me one
more time, I'm going to punch his capped teeth in."

Daniel gave her what could only be described as a
wryly warning look before saying, "I'm sure he didn't
mean anything by it, darling. He's just the friendly sort."

She watched in disbelief as he pulled a small electronic device from an inside pocket of his jacket and began to walk around the room with it. Having spent the past eighteen months working for her uncles, she figured out immediately what he was doing. Did he really think the rooms were bugged with listening devices?

Just what had she stumbled into here? What exactly had Daniel gotten involved with since he had left the Walker ranch foster home for at-risk teenage boys?

Chapter Two

Daniel motioned for B.J. to keep talking. She figured if Drake was eavesdropping on her, she was going to make it count. "He creeps me out. Obviously thinks he's God's gift to women—but the joke's on him. He's a slug."

Daniel rolled his eyes. Still speaking in a soothing, placating tone, he said, "Now, sweetheart, you're just tired. It has been a stressful day for you."

He could say that again. And then *again,* for emphasis.

She had told her uncles recently that she wanted more exciting and challenging assignments than the computer searches she had been doing for the past months. She had never imagined that this seemingly innocuous assignment would go so wildly off course.

Speaking of her uncles… "I need to call home."

Daniel returned from the bedroom, tucking his little spy gadget back into his pocket. Something about the way he walked told her all was clear even before he spoke. "We can talk freely now. At least, we can until we leave and return—at which point I'll sweep the rooms again, just to be on the safe side."

"I need to call home," she repeated. "But first… maybe you can tell me what the *hell* is going on?"

Grimacing in response to her renewed anger, he shrugged out of his jacket and tossed it over the back of the prissy white brocade sofa that matched the rest of the delicately fancy furnishings in the overdone room. Overdone in B.J.'s opinion, anyway. She preferred simpler, less ornate surroundings. Her idea of resort decor would have involved wicker and cotton, thick cushions and inviting ottomans.

Without directly responding to her, Daniel moved to the white-painted-and-gilded wet bar built into one corner of the room. He opened a small refrigerator and scanned the contents. "Would you like something to drink? We have sodas, juice and bottled water. Unless you need something harder—and I wouldn't blame you if you did, considering everything."

She started to curtly decline anything, but then she realized she really was thirsty. "I'll have a bottled water."

He carried one around to her, motioning for her to

sit down. She chose a chair that sacrificed comfort for style, perching on the edge of the seat with her water bottle clutched tightly in her hand.

She did not take her eyes away from Daniel's unrevealing face as he sat on the sofa opposite her, sipping soda and looking remarkably relaxed. How could he be so calm about this bizarre situation? And what exactly *was* the situation?

"I'm waiting," she reminded him. "I'd like to know what I'm doing here. Why you let them believe I'm your wife. I want to know what you're involved in—and why you seem so sure I'll be in danger if I tell the truth. Mostly I want to know when I can leave."

He took his time answering, and that only annoyed her more, as he seemed to be weighing his words. Deciding exactly what he could—or wanted—to tell her. "Two or three days," he said finally. "That should be all it will take."

"All it will take to do what? Damn it, Daniel, *talk to me!*"

He studied her face for a long moment, then absolutely floored her by chuckling. What on earth was there to laugh about?

"You've changed. You were so sweet-natured and easy to please. The perfect daughter, straight-A student, never caused any trouble, never said a cross word to anyone—except maybe your older brother and sister."

He remembered all that about her? She had been exactly the way he described her, back when he knew her. It was only within the past three or four years that she had become aware of how tired she was of pleasing everyone but herself. Of living a sheltered, uneventful, unadventurous life that had become increasingly stifling and boring.

She had wished for excitement. She should have remembered that old adage about being careful what one wished for.

"You still haven't answered my questions," she prodded gruffly.

Another brief hesitation and then he said, "I can't tell you much. Only that you've stumbled into a very complicated situation—as I assume you've figured out for yourself."

"Go on."

"Judson Drake thinks I have a wealthy wife back in Texas. He invited me to bring her along on this trip, but I had a convenient excuse to explain her absence. When you showed up at the farm, asking for me by name when no one should have known I was there—and asking with a very obvious Texas twang, by the way—Bernard put two and two together. I admit he isn't the sharpest thorn on the rosebush, but even he can handle that level of mathematics."

"So why didn't you tell him that I'm *not* your wife? As clever as you are," she said, adding an extra helping of sarcasm to her "Texas twang," "you should have been able to come up with some sort of explanation for my arrival. Say, oh, the truth, for example."

"Wouldn't have worked. My background, according to what Drake has been told, is one of upper-middle-class comfort. Private schools, public college, fortuitous marriage to a woman with money. Nowhere in that story is a mention of foster care. The truth about how I know you could have blown everything."

"So the wife is as fictional as your upper-middle-class background?"

His face expressionless again, he nodded.

"Why have you told them these things?"

"I can't go into that right now."

"You expect me to simply accept what you've told me and go along with this charade for the next two or three days?"

"I wish I could say you have the option of saying no. Unfortunately you don't. These are dangerous people, Brittany—"

"B.J."

"Sorry. B.J. These men will not accept a change in my story now. One hint that I've tried to deceive them, and you and I will both quietly disappear. That's how they operate."

"Then why are you here?"

He took a sip of his soda before saying, "There's a great deal of money involved for anyone who is clever enough to get a piece of it."

"Money?" She stared at him with narrowed eyes. "You're doing this for money?"

He shrugged and drained the remainder of his soda.

B.J. set her water aside. She simply didn't know whether she could believe a word he said.

She had thought he might try to tell her he was an

undercover operative for some branch of law enforcement. Would that have been any easier for her to believe? And if so, would it have been because she wanted to think Daniel was on the right side of the law?

"So what you're telling me," she said slowly, "is that you're running some sort of scam on some very dangerous men. And I'm stuck helping you pull it off because I accidentally arrived at the wrong place at the wrong time."

"That pretty well sums it up."

"If I refuse, I might just 'quietly disappear.' And if I agree, I could end up making some big mistake, and then we'll still end up dead."

"You won't make a mistake. All you have to do is remember a few details I'll tell you before we go out again."

"And what do I tell my family when I call them?"

"You can't call them. I don't trust either the land lines or the airwaves here. Either one could be monitored."

She shook her head. "You're going to have to figure out some way to let me call. Unless you want my uncles arriving in the middle of your big plan, of course."

Which didn't sound like such a bad idea to her, actually.

"How would they know where to find you? You didn't have time to call anyone when we left."

"For that matter, I don't know where we are exactly," she admitted. "But I wouldn't be particularly surprised if my uncles track me down within twenty-four hours. You do remember who they are, don't you?"

He frowned. "I'm well aware that your uncle Jared

is a rancher, since I spent nearly a year living with his family."

"And my uncles Tony, Joe and Ryan are private investigators. Very good ones. And very protective of all their family members—even one who is on their payroll. Me."

"You work for the D'Alessandro and Walker agency?"

"So you do remember them."

"Vaguely. It seemed like your family found an excuse nearly every week to have some sort of party at the ranch. I couldn't help but remember a few details about them."

"Then you should also recall that we're an extremely close family." Almost suffocatingly close sometimes, she almost added. "They'll start looking."

"You can send them an e-mail," he said after a moment. "I have a small computer in my luggage. You can use that. Don't keep a copy."

"And what should it say?" she asked.

"That you've decided you need a few days of vacation and they don't need to worry about you. You're twenty-seven years old. You don't have to ask permission to take a few days off, do you?"

He remembered an awful lot about her. Of course, she knew he was twenty-nine, because he was two years older than she, almost to the day.

"It's not something I've done before. Take off on impulse, I mean." Even though she had often wished she could.

"Then it's about time you did, wouldn't you say?"

"Maybe. But this wouldn't exactly be my first choice of vacations."

"Yeah?" Looking more masculine than he should have against the froufrou fabric, he stretched an arm along the back of the sofa. "So what would be your first choice?"

"Well…I don't know. I haven't really thought about slipping off on my own."

His beautifully shaped lips curved into a very slight smile. "Liar."

Okay, so maybe she had indulged in a few daydreams lately about getting away from the usual routines. "I guess I've thought about it once or twice," she muttered.

"To where?"

"Anywhere. I've hardly been out of Texas. I've always wanted to go someplace really different and exotic—like—like Singapore. Or Hong Kong. Or Bali."

And then she shook her head impatiently. "Darn it, you're doing it again. Distracting me from the questions you don't want to answer."

Still wearing that annoyingly inscrutable smile, he merely looked at her.

"Will you at least reassure me that I won't be helping you break the law if I stupidly agree to go along with this ridiculous charade?"

He never changed expression. Nor did he bother to say anything.

She scowled fiercely—not that she figured it would affect him. "So my choices are to cooperate with everything you say even though you won't tell me why or refuse to go along and risk having Bernard make me disappear."

"The options haven't changed since I first outlined them to you."

"Maybe it has taken me this long to make myself believe this is really happening," she grumbled.

"Since I assume you're choosing the option that keeps us both alive, we need to go over a few things."

Though B.J. couldn't help but resent Daniel's assumption that she would make the choice he wanted her to make, she couldn't really argue with him either. She had no wish to face the business end of Bernard's weapon. "I suppose you're right. If I'm to play a part, it would be helpful if I have a script."

A sudden thought occurred to her. "Wait a minute. Did you never mention your wife's name? You introduced me to Creepy Guy as B.J."

"That's not a problem."

Something in his voice struck her as odd, but he was speaking again before she could define it. "There's very little that you have to remember. We've been married for two years. You are a homemaker and community volunteer who leaves all business and financial matters to her husband."

"Oh, gee, thanks for making me such a progressive, modern woman."

He ignored her—something he did entirely too easily, she thought. "Last fall you suffered a miscarriage and you've been somewhat despondent since. You've had even less interest in my business dealings with your money, which means I'm free to speculate with it at my own discretion."

The more he told her, the less enthused she became with her role. A mopey housewife. Terrific. "I suppose I adore the ground you walk on?"

That seemed to fit in with the chauvinistic tale he had concocted.

He looked almost amused by her resigned question. "Of course. I've been the loving and solicitous husband since your loss. Which, of course, makes you less inclined to question my actions away from you."

"So you don't love me?" It felt foolish to ask that of a man who was a virtual stranger—but it was only a charade, after all, she reminded herself.

A tiny shiver slipped down her spine when his dark eyes held hers for a heartbeat before he replied. "I've implied to Drake that I love your money more."

She pulled her gaze from his, glancing down at her hands. "Then I would say you're in sorry shape, considering I don't have any."

"My wife has plenty of money," he corrected her.

The gold ring on her left hand glittered. She touched it with her right forefinger. "You just happened to have a woman's wedding ring on a chain around your neck? Just in case someone stumbled into your story?"

"The ring was my mother's. I've worn it for almost a dozen years."

Despite the utter lack of emotion in his voice, B.J.

felt her throat tighten anyway. She knew enough about his mother's fate to understand how much this ring must mean to him. He had carried it with him when he left the Walker ranch and he had worn it since as a reminder of—what? His mother's life? The injustice of her death?

"I'll take very good care of it," she assured him.

"Thank you." He stood then, glancing toward the bedroom. "Feel free to rest a while if you like. I'll make sure you aren't disturbed."

"Actually…" Rising, she put a hand to her midsection. "I'm starving. It's been hours since I've had anything to eat."

The smile he gave her then was quick and apparently genuine. "We can't have that. Room service or restaurant?"

Dragging her gaze from his amazing smile, she looked ruefully down at her wrinkled and travel-worn clothing. "Maybe room service would be best."

Following her gaze, he nodded. "What size do you wear?"

"Size two. Why?"

"Shoe size?"

"Seven. Why are you—?"

"You'll need some clothing."

He picked up a phone from an ornately carved and gilded writing desk. She listened in astonishment as he briskly and efficiently ordered a meal and then requested that an assortment of clothing, shoes and lingerie be sent to their suite for his wife's consideration. Despite what she knew about his impoverished background, he seemed to have adapted very well to a life of privilege.

Hanging up the phone, he moved toward the bedroom. "I'll set up the computer for you. You can send your e-mail while I unpack."

She followed him into the bedroom. This room, too, was overly formal for her taste. Done in French style, it featured carved woods and lots of chintz and toile on little chairs and benches that looked barely substantial enough to support her weight, much less Daniel's.

Whose idea of a vacation room was this? She couldn't see herself putting her feet up on this furniture or lolling around still damp and sandy from a romp on the beach. Did people who were comfortable in rooms like this even *like* romping on beaches?

Daniel chuckled again in response to her expression. "You don't care for the decor?"

It irked her that he read her so easily when she could never tell what he was thinking. She waved imperiously toward another French writing desk. "Set up the computer. I have an e-mail to write."

He reached for a leather computer case. "By the way," he said casually, "you won't be able to hit send until I've read the message. Sorry, but I have to make sure you stay safe while you're under my protection."

She lifted her chin defiantly. "I'll have you know I've been working for the investigation agency for over a year. I can keep myself safe."

"Since my guess is that you've been working primarily at a desk, doing computer searches and making telephone calls, I doubt that you've learned a great deal of self-defense during your stint at the agency."

Without giving her a chance to challenge his guess, he opened the computer, turned it on, then stepped back from it. "Let me know when you're ready, and I'll enter my code so you can send the e-mail. After I've read it, of course."

"Jerk," she muttered beneath her breath as she sank into the tiny chair in front of the desk.

Again he surprised her by laughing softly. "It's not the first time you've called me that," he reminded her. "I'm sure it won't be the last."

His voice grew more serious then. "But you will leave this resort safely. You have my word on that."

The message had been approved and sent by the time their early dinner arrived. Daniel had read every word carefully, weighing the implications and trying to predict her family's reactions to the e-mail. She had said simply that she had been unable to find Daniel and wanted to take a few days to think about her future. She had sent her love and promised to call soon.

"They all know I've been increasingly dissatisfied with my job lately," she had rather grudgingly admitted. "Sitting at a computer all day wasn't what I had in mind when I talked my uncles into giving me a job."

"Most P.I. work these days comes down to just that," he had observed with a slight shrug. "From what I've heard, anyway."

"So I've discovered."

"So what do you want to do?" he asked, discreetly keying in his computer password while he kept her distracted with conversation.

"I don't know," she answered simply. And rather poignantly. "I only know I haven't found it yet."

Barely twenty minutes later, he studied her across the small round dining table set against one glass wall in the sitting room. Apparently her confusion about the situation she had found herself in—coupled with a whirlwind day of travel—had not affected her appetite. She ate with a heartiness that amused him, considering her reed-slender figure.

He remembered that she had liked to eat when they were teenagers. She'd always been one of the first in line for helpings of the barbecued meats that had been the main fare of so many Walker family gatherings.

They didn't say much during the meal. He figured she was replaying the things he had said to her, trying to make sense of them and prepare herself for the role she'd been forced into assuming.

They had just dipped into their desserts when there was another knock on the door. Motioning for B.J. to continue to eat the strawberry shortcake she seemed to be enjoying so much, Daniel moved to answer.

A striking young woman in a brief red sarong-style sundress and sandals stood in the hallway next to a covered, wheeled garment rack. "Mr. Andreas?"

He couldn't help noticing the masses of sun-streaked blond hair, glossy, full lips, golden-tanned shoulders,

high, firm breasts and long, tanned legs. He was only
human, after all. "Yes."

Her smile glittered, as did her violet-tinted eyes.
Young Elizabeth Taylor eyes, he mused. He had no
doubt that tinted contact lenses provided the color, but
the result was quite nice. "I'm Heather. From the Beach-
front Boutique? I understand your poor wife arrived
without her luggage."

"Yes. An unfortunate airline mix-up." He turned toward the small dining area at the other side of the room.
"B.J.?"

She was already up and moving toward them. Her
short dark hair was mussed, any makeup she had worn
earlier had worn off and her slightly oversize camp shirt
and khakis emphasized her slender frame.

Many men, perhaps, would have preferred Heather's
more obvious feminine charms. Yet Daniel found himself increasingly fascinated by B.J.'s subtle—and completely natural—attractions.

"Heather, this is my wife," he said, helping her roll
the bulky garment rack inside. "Darling, I'm sure you'll
be glad to have some fresh clothing to change into."

He noticed that Heather was eying B.J. in surprise,
as if she had expected her to look different. Heather was
accustomed, he imagined, to very wealthy men with
sleek, ultragroomed eye-candy wives.

He didn't blame her for that expectation, of course.
When he had very briefly considered casting the role of
his "wife" for this trip, that was exactly the type of
woman he would have selected. Someone who looked

rich and pampered and a bit disconnected from the real world.

He had rejected the idea of bringing someone along because he was concerned that the situation would become too complicated. Too distracting.

He'd had no idea, of course, that fate would step in to provide a make-believe wife for him. And that fate's choice would be even more complicated and distracting than anyone else Daniel could possibly have found on his own.

Chapter Three

At Daniel's request, Heather left the clothing for B.J. to examine in private. She promised to return in an hour to collect the rack and invoice the selections.

When Heather departed, Daniel removed the cover from the wheeled rack. He motioned toward the colorful garments hanging from the top bar and neatly folded into clear plastic boxes fitted into the bottom part of the display rack. "There you are. A boutique on wheels, with everything in your size."

Hands on her hips, she looked from the rack to his decidedly smug expression. "You enjoy snapping your fingers and having people jump to please you, don't you?"

His eyebrows lifted, as if he was surprised that she had even to ask. "Of course."

"Just what have you been up to for the past thirteen years, Daniel?"

Displaying that annoyingly selective hearing again, he turned toward the clothing rack and plucked a hanger from the rod. "This would look good on you."

The yellow cotton sundress clipped to the hanger was strapless and short and tailored to fit very snugly. "That's not really my style."

"Yes, but remember, you're playing a new role here. You're wealthy, stylish and accustomed to designer fashions."

"According to your backstory, I'm depressed and too self-absorbed to even notice that you're frittering away my money. Would a person like that really wear skimpy, brightly colored dresses?"

"Ah, but you also adore the husband who treats you like delicate and valuable glass. You would certainly want to dress to please him."

She scowled, wondering if he was always so quick at coming up with counterarguments. Just once she would like to win one of their verbal skirmishes. "I don't like yellow."

"In that case…" He replaced the sundress and pulled out a similar one in deep fuchsia. "Is this better?"

"Maybe I should just select a couple of things for myself," she said, moving toward the rack.

"Since it's important that you present the image Drake is expecting, I feel compelled to assist you in your selections."

"And when did you start talking like that? That isn't

the way you used to talk when I knew you before. Back when you were Daniel Castillo," she couldn't resist adding.

She hadn't been surprised to learn from a reliable source that he was now using his mother's maiden name, but she wanted him to know that this masquerade hadn't erased from her mind the reality of who he had once been.

For just a moment his self-satisfied smile faded. She could almost see a few painful old memories swirl in his dark eyes before he hid again behind the bland mask he donned so easily. "Yes, well, you aren't the only one playing a role."

Changing the subject then, he pulled several garments from the rack, piling them into B.J.'s arms. "These look as though they would work for you. Why don't you take them into the bedroom and let's see how well they fit."

She peered at him over the huge pile of clothing. "You expect a fashion show?"

His faint smile back in place, he dropped onto the sofa and draped an arm over its curvy back. "I think I'd enjoy that."

She was strongly tempted to give him a suggestion he would not enjoy quite so much, but she bit her tongue to hold it back. For one thing, she wasn't one to use such language easily. For another, she had a glum suspicion that Daniel was right.

Given her own tastes in clothing, she would probably never pass for a wealthy socialite. Her poor mother had tried for years to talk her into dressing with more of an eye for fashion than comfort.

She sighed heavily. "When this is over, you are going to owe me big-time for saving your butt."

"Technically you're saving both our butts," he pointed out equably. "But when this is over, I will definitely owe you whatever penalty you choose to make me pay."

"I'm glad you agree. Thinking about that penalty will help me get through this ordeal."

He grimaced slightly, as though well aware of the punishments her imagination could conjure up. "Try on some clothes," he said. "You have less than an hour before Heather will be back."

Turning on one heel, she stamped into the bedroom, which wasn't easy when she could barely see over the pile of clothing she carried. Daniel didn't offer to assist her. He probably knew she would have snarled at him had he tried.

Daniel turned out to be surprisingly difficult to please. While B.J. would have just grabbed the first things that fit, he seemed to have a shrewd eye for what suited her best, rejecting the outfits that hung too loosely on her slender frame or were less than flattering to her skin tone. She was beginning to feel like a mannequin by the time he finally approved a couple of sundresses—including the fuchsia one—several summery capri-pants-and-top sets and one classic black sheath.

"This is too much," she protested. "We aren't going to be here that long."

"You never know," he replied with a shrug. "Besides, the clothes look good on you. You should keep them."

"And who's paying for them?" she asked tartly.

"That needn't concern you."

"And yet it does."

"Just try on the bathing suits, B.J."

"No way am I modeling bathing suits for you."

He heaved a long-suffering sigh. "Then pick a couple for yourself. You can't stay at an oceanside resort without a bathing suit or two. And be sure you keep enough nightclothes and lingerie for several days."

She started to snap at him that she was perfectly capable of providing herself with lingerie, but she bit the words back. She just couldn't discuss underwear with Daniel, even if it was in defiance. Besides which, she did need some clean undergarments if she was going to stay here even for just two or three days.

Turning silently, she closed herself in the bedroom to complete her shopping without any further input from Daniel.

Heather had just left with the garment rack later when someone else knocked on the sitting room door. Since the dishes from their meal had already been cleared away, B.J. looked curiously at Daniel. "Now what?"

He shrugged and crossed the room to answer. She found herself thinking that he moved like a man braced for trouble, as if he half expected danger to lurk on the other side of the door.

She couldn't help wondering again just what he had been up to for the past thirteen years. She'd been able to find out very little about him through the usual sources.

He glanced through the peephole, relaxed visibly and opened the door. A moment later he closed the door again and turned back to face her. His arms were filled with a gigantic gift basket covered in cellophane and topped with a glittering golden bow. "It's for you."

"For me?" Frowning, she moved toward him as he set the basket on a table.

Through the clear covering she could see that the basket was filled with beauty products. Body lotions, cleansers, moisturizers, sunscreens. An assortment of cosmetics. Dainty little soaps. Hair products, including a brush and a hand mirror.

She spotted a clear plastic case fitted with a toothbrush, toothpaste, mouthwash, a razor and a pink can of shaving gel. Everything a woman on vacation could possibly need. She had never cared much about brand names, but she suspected that the products in this basket were top-of-the-line.

"Did you order this, too?" she asked Daniel.

He shook his head and pulled a tiny card from a fold in the cellophane. The card bore the gold-embossed name of a resort gift shop. He held it so both could see the words as he read aloud, "'Not that you need any enhancement, but perhaps these things will be of use to you during your stay. Please ask for anything else you need. Judson Drake.'"

B.J. wrinkled her nose. "Eew."

Daniel shook his head. "You're going to have to get

past that tendency to shudder every time you hear his name. He's our host, and I'm trying to very hard to take him for a large amount of money. A little kissing up would definitely be in order."

B.J. shuddered again. "If either of us is expected to kiss Creepy Guy, it had better be you."

Reaching out to run a fingertip across her pouting lower lip, he murmured, "He's not my type."

Her mind flooded suddenly with memories of the kiss with which he had greeted her at the farmhouse— had that really been less than eight hours ago?; it seemed longer—and yet she could still almost feel the warmth of his lips against hers.

Dropping his hand, he glanced at the wrinkled clothes she had donned again after trying on the new outfits. "Why don't you put on one of those new dresses and we'll go out for a drink and to listen to some music. We should let ourselves be seen."

She gave it a moment's thought. She had a choice of going out for a drink or sitting in this suite with him— just the two of them—for the remainder of the evening. "A drink sounds good," she said—perhaps just a bit too hastily.

He flashed her a smile. "I'll freshen up after you change. It won't take me long."

Nodding, she turned toward the bedroom, leaving him gazing out the big window toward the darkening beach beyond. It was definitely a good thing she had chosen to go out, considering the way her hands were shaking merely in response to his lethal smile.

* * *

The sun had set by the time they went out, though the temperature was still pleasantly warm. Feeling as though she were playing dress-up, B.J. wore the fuchsia dress. The garment was a much brighter color than she would have chosen for herself, the bodice too low-cut, the hem too high. While she supposed it was fairly modest compared to some of the outfits she saw when they entered the rather crowded outdoor lounge, she would have been much more comfortable in jeans and a T-shirt.

Because it had seemed almost obligatory with the dress, she had even worn makeup for the evening, forcing herself to open the gift basket Drake had sent to the suite. She'd assured herself she didn't have to like him to take advantage of his generosity—especially since he probably had ulterior motives in making the gesture—but it still felt wrong somehow.

Daniel had told her she looked very nice. As usual, she hadn't been able to read his expression to judge whether he'd really meant the compliment or if he was only being polite. Glancing from beneath her eyelashes at the sleek, beautiful women occupying the candlelit little tables around them in the outdoor lounge, she couldn't help thinking that she must stand out among them like a plain brown sparrow in an exotic aviary.

Daniel, on the other hand, fit in very well with the glamorous crowd. His black hair still slightly damp from his quick shower, he wore a thin white shirt and loose cream-colored slacks that contrasted intriguingly with his dark skin and emphasized his long, lean body.

She noticed how many of the beautiful women—and a few of the beautiful men—turned to stare at Daniel as they crossed the stone floor to a rather isolated empty table. She wondered if it was only paranoia making her think she saw surprise in their eyes that a man like Daniel was with her.

"What's wrong?" he asked as he held her chair for her.

It bugged her that he sensed her moods so easily. "Nothing."

He pulled his chair so close to hers that their knees touched beneath the tiny table. "Appearances," he reminded her when she looked inquiringly at him.

"I'm not sure anything is going to make it appear that I belong at a place like this," she murmured, waving a hand around the lounge, with its smooth stone floor, low rock walls lined with waving palm trees and huge pots of tropical flowers, colorful overhead lanterns and dozens of flickering candles.

In the center of the circular lounge was a small bandstand on which a five-piece ensemble played sultry dance music. A wooden dance floor surrounded the bandstand, making it easily accessible from any table, and several bronzed, toned, bleached and designer-clad couples took advantage of the chance to show off their dancing skills. The place was a far cry from the beer-and-barbecue joints her solidly middle-class family tended to frequent back home in Texas.

Daniel frowned. "Why wouldn't you look as though you belong here?"

She shrugged self-consciously. "I would never be able to afford to stay at a resort like this on my own."

"That doesn't make you inferior to anyone here. Don't mistake money for class, Britt—B.J."

A pretty blonde in a sarong—which seemed to describe nearly every employee at this resort—stopped beside the table. "What would you like?"

"Darling?"

B.J. gave Daniel a look. It would serve him right—not to mention prove her point—if she ordered root beer. "Why don't you order for us, *darling?*"

His smile flashed, giving her just a fleeting glimpse of the shallow dimple in his left cheek. She remembered having a rather obsessive fascination with that elusive dimple when she was fourteen. "Champagne, then—since it's your favorite."

He glanced at the server and ordered a brand B.J. didn't recognize. Probably very expensive.

"Champagne is my favorite drink?" she murmured when the server moved away.

"It seemed to fit in character."

Because it was making her rather nervous to be sitting so close to him, gazing into his dark eyes, she forced herself to look away, turning her attention toward the bandstand. Reflections of the tiny white lights strung above them glittered like stars on the glossy grand piano and gleaming wind instruments.

Beneath the bluesy music she could just hear the

sound of the ocean. The scent of tropical blooms drifted past her on a light breeze. The slow swaying of the dancing couples was almost hypnotic.

The server returned with their champagne. B.J. took an appreciative sip before saying, "One thing I will say about Creepy Guy, he runs a nice place."

Though the corners of Daniel's mouth twitched, he glanced quickly around, silently reminding her that she had to be careful. "It does look nice," he murmured. "On the surface."

Yet another reminder that danger lurked beneath the exotic beauty here. Glancing around, she saw Bernard and another large man sharing a table near the stage. Though the men weren't looking her way, she had little doubt they had been aware of the moment she and Daniel arrived. She shivered.

Daniel slipped an arm around her, his shirt fabric very soft against the skin her dress left bare. "Cold?"

"No." Definitely not cold. Not now, anyway.

"We can speak freely—as long as we keep our voices low." He was practically nuzzling her temple as he spoke, so there was little danger of anyone overhearing him, even from the next table. The table he had selected was partially screened by the drooping fronds of a large potted palm, and she doubted that his selection had been made by accident.

She suspected that Daniel's every action was calculated and deliberate. Including the nuzzling.

"You should try to smile at me occasionally. Pretend to be intensely interested in what I have to say."

"Gaze adoringly into your eyes?" she suggested too sweetly.

He chuckled and brushed a kiss against her cheek. "That would certainly be helpful."

It was only the thought of Bernard sitting nearby and watching them that kept B.J. from jerking away. She was afraid it would take more acting talent than she possessed to pretend that the touch of Daniel's lips against her skin was an everyday occurrence for her. "I'll, uh, see what I can do."

"Relax, B.J. I'm not going to bite you. Yet."

Now he was deliberately trying to rattle her. "You always did have an irritating streak in you."

"You're still under the impression that I was the one who put the little snake in your bag?"

"I'm quite sure you were. I saw you busting a gut laughing when I screamed and threw that bag about twenty yards into the bushes."

His smile was a bit nostalgic. "It was amusing."

"Admit it. You did it."

When he merely looked at her, she frowned, a long-held belief beginning to waver. "It wasn't you?"

He shook his head.

"Then who...?"

Lifting his champagne flute, he murmured into it, "Far be it from me to squeal—but you might have a chat with your cousin Jason when you return home."

She narrowed her eyes, picturing her brilliant and unconventional cousin, Jason D'Alessandro. "Practical jokes aren't Jason's style. Now, if you had blamed my cousins Aaron and Andrew Walker, I might have believed you. The twins were always getting into mischief when they were kids. Heck, they're twenty-one now and they're still always up to something."

"I never figured out how you could keep all that family straight. How many cousins do you have, anyway?"

"My father was an only child with a small extended family. But my mother has five living siblings. Between them, and a brother who died years ago, they have fifteen offspring. Two of my first cousins, Shane and Brynn, have children of their own now."

"Shane's a father?" Because Shane was the son of the couple who had served as Daniel's foster parents, Daniel obviously remembered him well enough to be surprised.

"Yes. He and Kelly married only a couple of years after you left the ranch. They have two daughters—Annie, who's eight, and Lucy, who's four."

"Do they all still live at the ranch?"

She nodded. "Shane added on to his house when Lucy was on the way, but other than that, not much has changed since you were there."

"How are—" He broke off the question, took another sip of his champagne, then set his flute down. "Would you like to dance?"

Apparently he had decided to close that door to his past for now. Was it because he was concerned about being overheard—or was it that he simply didn't like to remember those days?

"I don't dance very well."

"Not a problem. Besides, Bernard and his friend seem to be waiting for us to do something. We shouldn't disappoint them."

She glanced involuntarily toward the table near the stage. Bernard was staring right at them now, making no attempt to pretend otherwise. He nodded when she looked his way and lifted his glass in a salute of sorts.

Though there was nothing at all threatening about his actions, she felt her stomach muscles clench anyway. "Actually I'm getting rather tired."

"Then we'll go back to our suite—after our dance." Daniel stood and held out his left hand to her, the gold band on his finger gleaming in the reflected light from the candle on their table.

In other words, he wasn't giving her a choice. Apparently he considered it important that Bernard see them dancing together. She laid her hand in his and allowed him to lead her to the dance floor.

He had been right—as always—when he'd said that it wouldn't be a problem that she wasn't an experienced dancer. He held her so closely and moved so slowly that all she had to do was sway in place along with him. He didn't have to remind her that they were being watched, but he gave her little choice except to cling to him as if there was no one else in the entire resort.

She felt his lips press against her cheek, and it was purely instinct that made her tilt her head to grant him freer access. It was better, she decided, to simply act without thinking for now. Every time she started wondering what Daniel was up to or why she hadn't made more of an effort to get herself out of this situation, her head started to hurt.

She had a nagging suspicion that she should be more anxious, less willing to cooperate with Daniel's instructions. She was still trying to convince herself that he was on the right side of the law. An undercover cop. A private investigator, maybe. She told herself he had been trying too hard to convince her that he was no better than the men he was here to do business with, which must mean the truth was just the opposite, right?

Or was she still operating under the influence of a girlhood infatuation? Unable to believe the worst of the boy she had never forgotten? The man who could make her pulse race with nothing more than a slight smile? Not to mention the way she was reacting to being held so closely against his long, lean, muscular body.

She had never before allowed her hormones to overcome her common sense—and this was a hell of a time to start.

Her cheek rested against his shoulder now. As the song was winding down, he reached up to tilt her face toward him. Before she could say anything, his mouth was on hers. The kiss effectively ended the dance, since it rendered her completely unable to move her feet.

"Now," he said when he lifted his head several long moments later, "we can go back to our suite."

Blinking dazedly, she realized that other couples were leaving the dance floor. No one seemed to be paying much attention to them, but if anyone had been, they probably saw a couple eager to be alone to continue where the kiss had left off.

As Daniel led her away with one arm holding her snugly against him, she knew that was exactly the impression he had intended to give.

B.J. looked rather pale as they reentered the suite a few minutes later. Motioning for her to remain quiet while he swept for listening devices, Daniel regretted again that she had been put into this position. She was dead on her feet, and no wonder, considering all she had been through that day.

He probably shouldn't have pressured her to go out for drinks and dancing, but he believed it had been a useful outing. It had definitely reinforced his tale that his "wife" was completely absorbed with him, so enthralled by his skillful wooing that she had no interest in anything else that went on around her.

Reassured that no one had been in to bug their suite while they were gone, he turned back to B.J. "You're exhausted. You need some sleep."

Nodding wearily, she took a few steps toward the bedroom, then froze when he moved to follow her. "Um…where are *you* going to sleep? On the sofa?"

Had it only now occurred to her that their charade of marriage included sharing a bedroom?

"It's a king-size bed," he pointed out, waving a hand in that direction. "We can both sleep in it without even bumping into each other during the night."

She looked from him to that big bed and back again. "I don't think so."

Reaching up to squeeze the back of his neck, he spoke with deliberate impatience. "Trust me, Brittany, you are entirely safe with me tonight. We can't risk anyone suspecting that our 'marriage' is anything other than what I've said, so we'll share the bed, but only for sleeping. I plan to crash for a couple of hours and then I have some work to do on my computer before I meet with Drake tomorrow."

B.J. flushed, and it wasn't hard to see that she had interpreted his tone to mean that he had no interest in taking advantage of sharing a bed with her. His use of the name she had answered to as a teenager had probably reinforced the impression that he saw her only as an inconvenient reminder of his past, still just a girl in whom he had no particular romantic interest.

It hadn't been true then and it wasn't now. But he saw no reason to share that with her. Once she recovered from her embarrassment, she should be much more comfortable sharing this suite with him if she was reassured that she didn't have to worry about him making unwelcome passes.

At least, he assumed they would be unwelcome. And if they weren't—well, that created a whole new set of problems.

She lifted her chin in a proud little gesture he knew very well and pushed a hand through her short hair, making it stand in defiant spikes around her heated face. "You can sleep wherever you like. I'm so tired I won't even notice you're in the same suite. And tomorrow, after we've both rested, I expect for you to find a way to get me out of this intolerable charade and back to my life as quickly as possible."

He nodded. "I'll wait in the sitting room until you're in bed. I'll try not to disturb you when I come in or when I get back up."

She nodded curtly and turned toward the bathroom. "By the way," she said over her shoulder, her voice still icy, "I really prefer to answer to B.J."

"I'll try to remember."

"Do that."

The bathroom door closed with a snap that almost made him wince.

Chapter Four

B.J. hadn't expected to sleep, but her body had other plans. Dressed in the most modest pajamas that had been made available to her, she slept heavily enough that she barely roused when Daniel lay down beside her maybe an hour after she turned in and she never knew when he got back up. Though she woke early—just before seven o'clock—he was already gone, only a slight indentation in his pillow as evidence that he was ever there.

It was hard to believe she had just spent an entire night in bed with Daniel Andreas. And slept through it. Whether from stress, exhaustion or both, she had simply gone unconscious.

She took a lengthy shower in the huge, ornately elegant bathroom. Afterward she applied a minimum of makeup, then dressed in one of the new outfits—a pale green sleeveless top with green-and-white-checked capris and green flip-flops. Studying herself in the mirror, she thought glumly that she looked like a soccer mom on her way to a PTA meeting. This was so not her.

Her gaze slid to the reflection of her left hand and the gold ring on her finger. Daniel's mother's ring.

She sank slowly to the edge of the bed, still looking at that ring. A simple gold band, it bore a few scratches that showed its age. It looked like what it was—a treasured memento.

Jarringly different mental images jockeyed for a moment in her mind.

Daniel at sixteen. Thin, dark, intense. Angry. Threadbare clothes, shaggy hair, conversation that consisted mostly of monosyllables and curse words.

Daniel at twenty-nine. Sleek, groomed, cultured. His emotions well hidden behind a blandly congenial social mask. In some ways it was hard to believe it was the same person.

And yet…

She remembered a glimpse of rarely seen dimple. A brief flash of amusement at the memory of a long-ago practical joke.

Perhaps he had changed outwardly, but he was still the boy who had broken down in front of her when he had talked about finding his mother's body. Did he remember that powerful moment as clearly as she did?

She would bet that he did. Maybe that was the reason he occasionally looked at her as though he would rather be anywhere other than with her now.

He entered the room so quietly that she didn't know he was there until he cleared his throat. She had never even heard the outer door open, which didn't reassure her about her safety in this luxurious suite.

As she rose to her feet, it was unexpectedly hard to meet his eyes. She kept remembering the boredom on his face when he had reassured her that he had no intention of making a pass at her during the night. He had all but told her outright that he wasn't attracted to her and that any evidence otherwise was merely an act he put on for the benefit of observers.

Even if he had only been trying to set her at ease about sleeping in the same room with him, it had been a fairly humiliating moment for her. She couldn't help thinking about the beautiful, busty blondes who seemed to have congregated at this resort. Perhaps they were more to Daniel's taste.

Not that she *wanted* to get involved with him, she assured herself hastily. He could be a criminal. At the very least, he was trouble.

"Good morning."

Pride made her force herself to meet his eyes. "Good morning."

"Did you sleep well?"

"Yes, quite well, thank you."

She didn't have to ask the same of him. She knew he hadn't had more than a few hours of sleep, but he looked

completely rested. His hair was neatly combed, his
cream-colored shirt and tan pants impeccably pressed.
Even though she was freshly showered and dressed and
wearing more makeup than she usually favored, he still
managed to make her feel slightly grubby in contrast to
him.

His dark eyes mocked her stilted tone. "You look
very nice."

She looked down at her neatly matched clothing. "I
look like a sitcom mom. All I need to finish off the look
is a string of pearls."

"Or this." He pulled a thin rectangular box from his
right pants pocket and extended it toward her.

Rather than taking it, B.J. eyed it suspiciously. "What
is that?"

"You won't know until you open it."

"I don't—"

He sighed and opened it himself, revealing a glittering diamond tennis bracelet. Each diamond was set in
a circle of hammered gold.

B.J. knew little about jewelry, since she usually wore
only a functional watch and a pair of diamond-stud earrings—half a carat each—her parents had given her for
her college graduation, but she would estimate this
bracelet to hold at least three carats of diamonds.

"You don't expect me to wear that?"

Daniel already had the bracelet out of its box. "I certainly do."

"Why?"

"Because Daniel Andreas was in such a good mood

62 **THE BORROWED RING**

after a night of romance with his wife that he stopped by the resort's jewelry store and picked up a bauble for her. Since certain people are undoubtedly aware of that purchase already, you should be seen wearing the bracelet. Preferably without a look of revulsion on your face."

"It isn't revulsion. The bracelet is certainly pretty. It just isn't…"

"It isn't you, I know." He caught her right hand in his left and wrapped the bracelet around her wrist. "Is it really necessary for me to remind you again that while you are here, you *aren't* you?"

Looking down at the bracelet he had fastened so easily around her wrist, she frowned. She didn't like the eerie feeling that she was slowly turning into someone else. Sure, she had wanted to make some changes in her life, but this was more drastic than she'd had in mind.

"So what are my orders for today?" she asked in resignation.

Maybe she had deliberately tried to annoy him— maybe because it made her so uncomfortable for him to stand so close to her, sliding diamonds onto her wrist. She should have predicted that he wouldn't be fazed by her sarcasm.

"You're staying at a luxurious oceanside resort. Take advantage of it. Lie by the pool. Walk on the beach. Shop in the boutiques. Spend the day in the spa. Have a massage and facial and manicure and pedicure. Or…" he reached up to brush his fingertips across her choppy hair "…visit one of the salons."

Embarrassed, she pushed his hand away. So she

hadn't had time to make a hair appointment lately. She had resorted to hacking at it occasionally herself, just to keep it out of her eyes. Still, she didn't think it looked all that bad. "Maybe I'll just stay here in the suite and watch the soaps on TV."

"Actually I think it would be best if you go out—at least for a little while. Be seen, flash your bracelet, act as though you're accustomed to being treated like a VIP."

"I thought I was supposed to be all depressed and stuff."

He smiled briefly at her wording but answered seriously. "You have been depressed, but you're responding well to my devoted attentions."

"Dancing and diamonds, for example."

"For example," he agreed.

"And while I'm flitting about the resort, basking in the afterglow of your attentions, what will *you* be doing?"

"I have business to conduct with our host."

"And you aren't going to tell me what that business is?"

He brushed a kiss across her temple. "Nothing for you to worry your pretty little head about."

"I want a divorce," she said in disgust.

That made him laugh and step back. "You'll have an annulment as soon as I can safely arrange it."

"Good."

"You must be hungry. Are you ready for breakfast?"

She shrugged. "I could eat."

He motioned toward the door. "There's a breakfast buffet in the restaurant downstairs. It looked pretty good when I walked past."

She looked wistfully toward the little dining table in their suite, but she suspected Daniel had a reason for wanting to go out. As she had noted before, Daniel seemed to have a reason for everything he did.

Saying the breakfast buffet looked "pretty good" had been an understatement. B.J. had never seen so much food spread in one place—outside a Walker family pot-luck, anyway.

Watching the scantily clad woman in front of her place a single strawberry and a half slice of whole-wheat toast on a tiny plate, B.J. shook her head and reached for a serving spoon. Her own plate was satisfyingly full when she carried it to their table a few moments later.

She hesitated only briefly when she saw that Daniel was already seated—and that he had been joined by Judson Drake. Her appetite decreasing significantly, she slipped into her chair and set her plate in front of her, giving Drake a perfunctory nod of greeting.

"Good morning, Mrs. Andreas." Drake had risen when she arrived and he took his seat again after she was seated.

"Mr. Drake."

"I hope you're enjoying your stay with us."

"It's a beautiful resort." That, at least, was true.

He glanced at her well-filled plate. "It's always a pleasure to see a woman appreciate our chef's efforts."

She really detested this guy. Even though he was being perfectly congenial, there was just something about him that made her want to punch him. And she had never considered herself a particularly violent woman.

She filled her mouth with Belgian waffle to avoid having to respond to him.

Her movement drew his eyes to the glittering new bracelet on her right wrist. "Very pretty," he said, touching it with his fingertips. "Though not as beautiful as its wearer, of course."

His fingers lingered a bit longer than necessary against her skin. She couldn't get over the nerve of this guy. He seemed so convinced that he could charm his way past the cool reserve she had shown around him. And it didn't seem to deter him in the least that Daniel was sitting only a few feet away.

"Thank you," she said and drew away from him to turn toward Daniel with a brilliant and—she hoped—adoring smile. "My husband gave it to me. He's such a sweet man."

"Sweet," Drake murmured, looking rather quizzically toward Daniel. Apparently the man he knew as Daniel Andreas was anything but "sweet."

Daniel took B.J.'s left hand and lifted it to his lips. "That's me," he murmured against her knuckles. "Just a sweet guy."

His gaze locked with B.J.'s over her hand, and she found herself unable to look away. His eyes were so dark, so reflective that she could almost see herself in them. If she didn't know better, she could almost believe that he very much liked what he saw.

"Well…" Sounding only slightly less affable than before, Drake stood. "I'll leave you lovebirds to your breakfast. Daniel, I'll see you in my office at ten. And by the way—all the times you talked about your lovely Brittany before? You hardly did her justice."

With what B.J. considered an especially oily smile, he nodded and moved on.

"That is the creepiest man I have ever met," B.J. muttered furiously.

"He's just—"

"Wait a minute." She set her fork down with a thump and frowned at Daniel. "He called me Brittany."

"Yes. Well, he doesn't know—"

"He said you talked about me—about Brittany—before we even came here yesterday. Or did I misunderstand?"

Daniel sighed in what sounded like resignation. "You didn't misunderstand. When I mentioned my wife to Drake before, I called her Brittany. Fortunately he seems to accept that I use your nickname when we're together."

"You made up a wife named Brittany?"

He glanced around to make sure no one could overhear them before replying in a low voice. "When I thought of a woman from Texas, the name Brittany just popped into my head. I suppose it was an old memory—besides, it sounds like the name of a woman from Texas with plenty of money."

"Which is why I prefer my initials," she muttered. "My mother gave me a name that's never felt like my own. Still—"

Daniel reached for his coffee mug, his face revealing none of his emotions. "The fact that I coincidentally used your name means nothing, of course. It has simply made it easier for us in the long run."

Taking the hint that he didn't want to talk about it anymore, she forced her attention back to her breakfast. Perhaps it truly meant nothing that he had given her name to his fictional wife. But it was very…interesting that he had done so, she mused.

B.J. went outside later that morning, not so much because Daniel had asked her to but because the maids were impatient to clean the suite and she didn't want to get in their way. She drifted through a few shops, but the merchandise displayed for purchase couldn't hold her attention.

There were quite a few people sitting around the pools, sunning, reading, tapping on laptop computers, but few were actually swimming. The tennis courts were in use, as were many of the machines in the workout facilities, but B.J. had no interest in either activity.

She settled finally for a long walk on the beach. She hadn't visited the ocean many times, and it was a pleasant diversion to stroll on the sand, letting the breeze stroke her skin and listening to the sounds of the surf. She walked slowly, stopping often to examine busy tide pools and interesting shells and to watch in delight as a few dolphins played in the waves some distance from the shore.

When the dolphins disappeared, she turned and began to walk again, farther from the resort. She saw a couple on horseback far ahead of her but passed no one else. Apparently this wasn't a popular swimming or sunning area, since the crowds seemed to have gathered closer to the resort, where umbrellas and cold drinks were at hand for their convenience.

The riders had turned and vanished, presumably taking another path back to the resort stables. Looking ahead, B.J. saw only sand and grass and rocks. If she continued walking, she would surely reach another resort. Some private beach homes, perhaps.

With a little luck—and a few phone calls—she could be back in Dallas by the end of the day, back to her own life. Leaving Daniel behind to somehow explain how his wealthy and gullible "wife" had suddenly disappeared. Her bolting would certainly make his story of domestic bliss look suspicious, and Drake would immediately begin to question everything else Daniel had told him.

If she had been told the truth, Drake would then arrange for Daniel to "quietly disappear." To be killed, in other words.

Her steps slowed and then stopped.

She didn't know what Daniel was doing. Which side of the law he was on. Whether anything he had told her was true. Whether she was endangering herself by staying with him. She didn't even know that he was really in danger himself.

She tried to tell herself it wasn't her problem. He was a grown man. He could take care of himself. For all she knew, it would be a relief to him if she removed herself from his life.

But what if he really was killed if she took off? Even though she would probably never know if her actions could cause such a thing, the uncertainty and guilt would haunt her forever.

She looked down at her left hand. At his mother's ring.

"Damn it." With a huge sigh, she turned on one heel to return to the resort.

Trudging doggedly back the way she had come, she called herself a fool. An idiot. A gullible, reckless moron. A—

"Mrs. Andreas."

Bernard had seemingly appeared from nowhere, materializing in front of her with a suddenness that made her gasp and fall back a step. "Where did you—"

"I'm sorry if I startled you," he said smoothly, his eyes gleaming with an amusement that belied the apology. "I thought you saw me approaching."

Which was a lie. He had known exactly what he was doing. Keeping that awareness to herself, she allowed her hand to flutter around her throat and said with a little laugh, "No, it's my fault. I was daydreaming and I completely lost track of my surroundings."

"You've wandered quite a way from the resort."

"Have I?" Absently fingering the diamond bracelet, she wrinkled her nose. "My husband says I live in my own world half the time. I have a terrible habit of getting lost in thought—and then getting physically lost as a result."

His gaze dropped to the bracelet and his thin lips curled in a cynical smile. "I'm sure you had quite a lot to think about. Are you on your way back to the resort now?"

"Yes. I believe I'll read by the pool this afternoon. The main pool is so lovely, with the waterfalls and tropical flowers. It's almost like being in the islands, don't you think?"

"Er, yeah, I think that's what the boss had in mind when he designed it."

"How clever of him. I must be sure and compliment him when I see him again." She moved past him, then looked inquiringly back over her shoulder. "I'm sorry, I forgot to ask. Were you looking for me for a reason?"

"Oh, uh, no, I—actually I wasn't looking for you at all. Just taking a walk on the beach."

The smile she gave him then was deliberately vague. "It's a lovely day for it. Have a nice stroll."

"Yeah. Thanks. See you around, Mrs. Andreas."

She walked much more quickly than she had earlier, the attractions of the beach no longer claiming her attention.

Bernard had been following her. Had she not decided to return to the resort, would he have allowed her to follow through with her urge to run?

Something told her the answer was no.

Chapter Five

Daniel found B.J. in the suite much later that afternoon, almost dinnertime. She was curled in a chair with a book, which she must have picked up in the gift shop downstairs, but she didn't seem to have read much of it.

He did his habitual electronics sweep and then asked her, "Have you been out?"

"I went for a walk earlier," she answered, tossing the paperback aside. "I couldn't enjoy it for the annoying shadows."

"Shadows?" he repeated, momentarily confused.

"One particular shadow named Bernard."

Daniel frowned. "He followed you?"

"Yes."

"Where?"

"I walked on the beach. I went quite a long way, actually."

Just how far had she intended to go? "And he stopped you?"

B.J. shook her head. "I had already turned back when he spoke to me."

He wasn't sure whether relief or surprise was uppermost in his mind when he asked, "What did he say to you?"

"He merely commented that I'd gone a long way from the resort. I did my best airhead impersonation and told him I'd been daydreaming and walked farther than I intended. And then I came back here. That was pretty much the extent of it. I, um, haven't been in the mood to go back out."

He squeezed the back of his neck. "Bernard won't hurt you as long as he doesn't suspect anything."

She didn't look particularly reassured. "I hate being watched. Especially without being aware of it."

"He was probably just curious about where you were going."

She gave him a seething look. "It was none of his business."

Sinking onto an ottoman near her chair, he clasped his hands loosely between his knees and studied her face. "So you had already turned around? Before you knew Bernard was watching you?"

She glanced down at her hands. "Yes."

"How tempted were you to keep walking?"

That brought her eyes back up to his. "Very."

"What made you change your mind?"

Her scowl told him she wasn't going to directly answer that question. Instead she asked, "Would Bernard have stopped me if I'd kept walking?"

"Yes," he replied simply, and he didn't imagine he needed to tell her that Bernard would have used whatever means necessary to do so.

"Then I guess it's a good thing I turned back, isn't it? Whatever my reasons."

She had tried to speak offhandedly, but the faint quiver in her voice confirmed that she hadn't needed the details.

The certainty that she had returned for his sake roused feelings in him he didn't want to examine too closely at the moment. He hadn't thought to warn her not to try to leave the resort while he was meeting with Drake; he'd thought he'd made it clear before that she wouldn't be allowed to leave. The fact that he hadn't reminded her again and that his carelessness could have gotten her—and perhaps him—killed made his stomach clench.

"I promised I would keep you safe," he reminded her. "But *you* have to be careful, too."

Her chin lifted. "I *have* been careful. And I'm fully capable of keeping myself safe."

"I know that." He reached out to take her hands in his. "You simply don't have experience with men like these, B.J. You can't imagine how dangerous they can be."

"I imagined clearly enough what they would do to you if I suddenly disappeared."

His fingers tightened around hers for a moment, and

then he said gruffly, "I can take care of myself, too. But thank you for caring."

"I'm not sure that I do care about the *man* who got me into this mess. But maybe I still care—a little—about the boy I used to know."

Sometimes her frankness caught him off guard, slipping beneath the thick barriers he had erected around his emotions. It was a trick she had first demonstrated thirteen years ago, when they were both just kids—and it seemed she still possessed the talent.

"That boy doesn't exist any longer," he told her.

She looked at him so intently that he almost squirmed, wondering what she saw. "What happened to him?" she asked finally.

A dozen years worth of images flashed through his mind, and few of them were pleasant ones. "Life happened."

"Daniel, tell me what you've been doing since you left the ranch."

"Surviving." He gave her hands another gentle squeeze, then released her and stood. "We should get ready for dinner. I'll wait out here while you change."

"We have to go out? We can't eat in here?"

Though he would have liked very much to give in to the plea in her eyes, he shook his head regretfully. "I'm afraid we have a dinner engagement."

She winced. "Please tell me we don't have to eat with Creepy Guy."

"I'm afraid we do. I'm sorry, I'll try to get us away early."

B.J. was on her feet and shaking her head, her expression turning mulish. "Tell him I have a headache and can't join you this evening."

"I need you to do this with me, B.J. Please."

For a moment he thought she was going to refuse—and short of carrying her bodily downstairs, there was little he could do to force her to accompany him. But then she sighed and pushed a hand through her hair. "Damn it."

He knew better than to smile at her disgruntled expression. "Is that a yes?"

She jabbed a finger into his chest—hard enough to leave a dent. "Your debt to me is mounting—and be warned, I fully intend to collect."

"I have no doubt that you will."

B.J. wore the little black dress for dinner. Sleeveless and fitted, with a moderately deep V neckline, it looked good on her—but it was the color that seemed to suit her mood best that evening. Just the thought of dining with Creepy Guy Drake made her want to dress in black.

Daniel's charcoal jacket was only a shade lighter than her dress, but his white shirt and light gray pants lightened it up. Studying him as he ran a comb through his glossy dark hair, she decided maybe the evening wouldn't be a total washout as long as she had Daniel to look at.

"You were a pretty teenager," she commented with a tilt of her head, "but you're even better-looking now. I guess that comes in handy for a con man."

She was amused when he dropped the comb. "You say the damnedest things."

She shrugged, rather pleased with herself for rattling him. "Just stating facts."

Turning toward her, he crossed his arms over his chest. "Actually you were a rather gangly child last time I saw you. All braces and legs and elbows."

Now it was her turn to be self-conscious—as he had no doubt intended. "I never claimed to be a beauty," she said gruffly.

"And I never thought you would turn into one." And then he smiled and cradled her face between his hands. "But damned if you didn't anyway."

She felt a flush start somewhere around the hollow of her throat and work its way up to the roots of her hair. "Stop that. We both know I'm not…"

"No. You're the only one who has doubts about your attractiveness." His right thumb moved against her cheek, pausing very close to the corner of her mouth. "As for myself, I've spent the past forty-eight hours trying not to notice how desirable you are. And failing miserably, I might add."

Her heart was suddenly racing, her pulse fluttering so rapidly in her throat that she could hardly speak. But he was simply trying to get back at her for embarrassing him—and he was doing a darned good job of it. "Now you're just being irritating again."

"Actually I'm being lamentably honest." He kissed the end of her nose, then dropped his hands and stepped back. "We'd better go. The sooner we get started, the sooner we can come back to the suite."

And when they did return, B.J. thought, turning rapidly toward the door, she was going to lock herself in the bedroom and leave Daniel to fend for himself.

Drake was already waiting for them in the resort's most formal restaurant. The table to which B.J. and Daniel were escorted was located at one end of the main dining room, slightly elevated and surrounded by a glass-brick half wall that screened but did not completely conceal it. The table overlooked the other diners and was serenaded by a small orchestra that faced that way. The crystal chandelier hanging over Drake's table was slightly more elaborate than all the others.

The overall impression was that of royalty, as though Drake and his guests were somewhat superior to the other diners. B.J. was embarrassed to be taken there.

Drake wasn't alone. He rose to greet his guests, then turned to his companion, a statuesque blonde—of course—with a flawless face and spectacular figure. "Daniel and Brittany Andreas, allow me to introduce Ingrid Jorgensen."

Without glancing at Drake, B.J. smiled politely at the other woman, who looked rather bored. "Please call me B.J."

The woman's very thin eyebrows rose a fraction of an inch. "B.J.?"

"My initials. They seem to suit me better than my first name."

Ingrid seemed to lose interest somewhere in the middle of the brief explanation. Or perhaps she'd had so many facial injections she was unable to express emotion, B.J. mused. And then chided herself for being catty as she allowed Daniel to hold her seat for her.

She wasn't usually the type to be threatened by stunningly beautiful women. Maybe Daniel was right that being in this place had triggered an insecurity response in her.

She couldn't help remembering that moment in the suite when Daniel had held her face in his hands and called her a beauty. Could he really say the same thing now that he saw her side by side with the breathtaking Ingrid?

Drake was seated at one side of the small round table with Ingrid on his left, B.J. on his right and Daniel directly opposite him. He turned to B.J. with one of his genial-host smiles. "I hope you had a pleasant day?"

"Lovely," she replied, letting her return smile show teeth. "I had a nice long walk on the beach." As he undoubtedly knew, she figured, since he had instructed his guard dog Bernard to follow her. "And then I relaxed for several hours with a good book."

He probably knew she'd charged the book to her room, too. Not that she could attest to it being a good book. She hadn't been able to concentrate enough to read more than a few pages.

"I've taken the liberty of ordering our meal in advance," Drake said when several servers arrived with trays of appetizers. "I believe my chef has prepared something for every taste."

Daniel replied, "I'm sure we'll enjoy the meal. We aren't picky eaters, are we, darling?"

B.J. turned a saccharine-sweet smile toward him. "Unless you count your unfortunate lactose intolerance." She turned to add chattily to Ingrid, "Poor dear walks the floor for hours after he eats dairy. Just like my grandfather used to do," she added with a sigh.

Ingrid looked vaguely horrified by the excess of information. Daniel stopped himself from reaching for a cheese cube and plucked a stuffed mushroom from the appetizer tray instead. The look in his eyes promised B.J. retribution, but he took some revenge by saying, "And my wife is deathly allergic to chocolate. Other than that, we'll eat just about anything."

Oh, low blow, she fumed. Especially when Drake patted her hand and said, "I'm glad to know that. I ordered chef's special chocolate lava cake for dessert. I'll have something else brought out for you, B.J. A bowl of fresh fruit, perhaps?"

Repressing a wistful sigh—chocolate lava cake sounded like the one thing that could even slightly salvage this evening—she nodded. "That sounds very nice."

Daniel would pay for that, she promised herself. It didn't even matter that she had fired the first shot.

"Tell us about yourself, B.J.," Drake encouraged during their second course. "Daniel and I have been doing all the talking this evening."

B.J. and Ingrid had eaten quietly, neither paying much attention to the men's discussion of current world events. B.J. was usually an active participant in mealtime conversations, but she had no particular interest in anything Drake had to say. "I'm afraid there's nothing interesting to tell you about myself. Perhaps Ingrid would like to share something with us?"

"Actually," Ingrid said, looking up from her barely touched food with the first sign of animation all evening, "I'm a singer. Well, I work as a runway model now, but I hope to…"

"Your husband has told me you're active in several charities," Drake said to B.J. as if Ingrid had never spoken. Ingrid subsided into silence again when he continued, "I suppose you're on the board of several foundations back in Texas?"

Easily checked on the Internet if she claimed that she was. "I've always been rather phobic about maintaining my privacy. I prefer to make my contributions behind the scenes."

Noting that Daniel gave her a look that approved her answer, she turned back to the sullen Ingrid. "I would like to hear more about your career as a model and a singer. That sounds so glamorous compared to my quiet life. What type of music do you sing?"

Glancing rather defiantly at Drake, Ingrid replied, "I love country music. Like Faith Hill and Shania Twain."

A country singer named Ingrid Jorgensen would certainly be a change, B.J. thought with a stifled smile. "I would love to hear you sing. Will you be performing here at the resort?"

The look Ingrid gave Drake this time was definitely resentful. "No."

"With all the venues available to you?" B.J. glanced at Drake in exaggerated astonishment. "I'm surprised."

Drake looked decidedly displeased, despite his forced smile. "I'm afraid not many of my guests are fans of country music."

"I wouldn't be so certain. Country music is quite popular with a broad range of listeners, I assure you."

"That's what I've been telling him," Ingrid said eagerly. "Just because he doesn't like country music, he thinks no one else does either."

"You must understand that Mrs. Andreas is from Texas, Ingrid. Musical tastes are a bit…different there."

"But appreciation for a beautiful, talented woman is universal," Daniel inserted smoothly, giving Ingrid a smile. "I, too, would enjoy hearing you sing…being from Texas myself."

The reproof was subtle but definitely there. Daniel had just made it clear that he would tolerate no insult—not even an implied one—against his wife.

Whatever the connection or power structure between Daniel and Drake, the latter backed off with a nod. "Of course. Ingrid, perhaps you'll work up a number with the band at the Seaside Lounge for tomorrow evening."

"I'd like that," Ingrid all but purred.

Still smiling with gritted teeth showing, Drake reached for his wineglass, giving B.J. a long look over the rim.

"I think you've made a new friend for life," Daniel commented later. "Ingrid practically kissed your hand when we parted."

Remembering the look in Drake's eyes when he had bade her good-night, B.J. swallowed. "I think I made an enemy, as well. Creepy Guy obviously doesn't like it when women challenge him. He was annoyed enough already that I didn't swoon every time he gave me one of his oily smiles."

The moon was full as they walked on the beach, providing them plenty of illumination. Yet B.J. was unable to read Daniel's expression. "Don't worry about Drake. There's a good chance we'll be out of here by this time tomorrow and you'll never have to see him again."

She wondered if she would ever see Daniel again after they left here. "We're leaving tomorrow?"

"I said there's a good chance. It depends on a couple of developments."

"What sort of developments?"

She didn't really expect him to answer, and he didn't. Instead he shrugged out of his jacket and draped it over her shoulders. "Is that better?"

She hadn't realized she was chilly until she felt the warmth of his jacket on her bare arms. The soft fabric smelled like Daniel, she realized as she drew the jacket more tightly against the cool ocean breeze. The scent was subtle, spicy, somewhat mysterious. A fanciful woman might have believed it carried just a hint of danger.

B.J. was trying very hard not to be fanciful tonight. "Thank you."

The moon hung low in the sky behind him, making his shirt gleam almost ghostly white but throwing his face into deep shadows. "You're welcome."

The walk had been Daniel's suggestion. She suspected he wanted to establish a pattern, making it look as though strolls on the beach were commonplace for her—probably to further weaken any curiosity about her trek that morning.

She doubted that he was deliberately procrastinating about returning to the suite. Despite his joke earlier, Daniel had no reason to be concerned about them being alone for another night.

She was the one who had to fret about fighting an unwelcome attraction. Impulses that could lead her into a world of trouble if she gave into them. An infatuation that had begun rather innocently more than a dozen years ago and was now complicated by wholly adult lust.

Despite his outrageous flirting with her earlier—which, she had no doubt, had been intended as an effective way to distract her from inconvenient questions—she didn't believe for a minute that Daniel worried about losing control of his impulses if they spent too much time alone together. For one thing, she couldn't believe that Daniel ever lost control.

They weren't the only ones out on this beautiful evening, but no one seemed to be paying them any attention. Most of the others were couples wrapped up in each other, staying as far away as possible from anyone else. Yet B.J. had the uncomfortable sensation that she and Daniel were being spied upon anyway. The fact that she couldn't spot the watchers made the suspicion even more unsettling.

Daniel draped an arm loosely around her shoulders, pulling her close enough to walk comfortably beside him yet still allow them to converse in very low voices. She knew better than to read anything personal into his action. She wasn't the only one aware of unseen observers.

"You never told me why you came looking for me in Missouri," he said from out of the blue.

"Sure I did."

"No. I'd have remembered."

She thought back over the past couple of days with him—and realized that he was right. She had never actually gotten around to telling him the reason she had tracked him down. "I guess I've been sort of…distracted."

"Understandable. So…?"

"I came to invite you to a party."

Obviously not what he had expected. He actually stumbled a step in the sand before he repeated, "A party?"

"A surprise twenty-fifth anniversary party for Uncle Jared and Aunt Cassie. It was their daughter Molly's idea. She's trying to gather most of the foster sons who have lived on the ranch during the past twenty-five years. She's located most of them, but you and a couple others pretty much dropped out of sight after you left."

"Frankly I'm surprised you found me."

"It wasn't easy—especially since you've changed your last name. But I remembered that you once told me you were considering switching to your mother's maiden name after you left the ranch." The slight uptilt she added to the end of the comment turned it into a subtle question.

He shrugged against her shoulder. "I created a false identity for Drake using my mother's name, thinking it wouldn't be a problem, since that wasn't the name I used as a boy, in case he checked."

"You used my name, too," she reminded him.

"Um, yeah. As I said, that was an odd coincidence."

"Hmm."

"So—all of this was over a party."

"A *big* party," she felt compelled to add. "Dozens of people will be there."

"And that's just your family."

The dry comment made her giggle. "Well…yeah. But other people, too. Uncle Jared and Aunt Cassie have touched a lot of lives during the past twenty-five years."

"I'm sure they have."

B.J. looked rather fiercely at the waves cresting white-topped in the moonlight. "I, um, thought they changed your life, too. At least, that's what you told me the day you left."

"That was a long time ago," he said after a moment.

"Do you remember what you said to me that day? You told me you were going to make something of yourself and then you would come back to thank the Walkers for all they had done for you."

"Like I said—it was a long time ago. I was just a kid. I barely remember those days—and I would be surprised if they remembered me."

"Of course they remember you, Daniel. You were a

part of their lives for a full year. They still have your photograph displayed with the other foster boys who have stayed with them and they mention you often when reminiscing about the past."

He remained silent.

"They would love to see you again," she ventured.

Without glancing at her, he murmured, "You really think they would be proud to learn that I've become a con man?"

"Is that what you are?"

"It's what you called me earlier," he reminded her.

"Was I right?"

"Oh, yeah. You were right about that."

She chewed on her lower lip, trying to interpret his tone and not his words. "Won't you at least tell me why you're here?"

"I've told you that already. I'm here for the money."

There was a ring of truth in his voice. As far as she knew, he hadn't actually lied to her yet. When she asked a question he didn't want to answer, he simply ignored it. So when he said he was here for the money, she supposed she should believe him.

"That's really it?" she couldn't help asking.

"If you're trying to find justification for my actions, forget it. I keep telling you, I'm not the kid you used to know."

His almost harsh tone contrasted with their still-cozy position. To an onlooker, they could have been murmuring sweet nothings to each other.

B.J. looked up at Daniel with a wistfulness she hoped

he couldn't see. Maybe he had changed, but he was wrong about her not being able to find justification— or at least explanation—for the man he had become. It made sense to her, in a way, that after a childhood of helplessness and deprivation, he would pursue power and wealth as an adult.

He had been angry then that extreme poverty had contributed to his mother's untimely death. He would be determined now not to allow himself to be at anyone's mercy again.

She had hoped, however, that he would seek his fortune through legitimate means. Education, career. Had his options really been so limited after he'd left the ranch—or had he only perceived them to be?

"Jared and Cassie wouldn't care what you've done since you left. They would still love to see you."

Perhaps there was just a note of wistfulness in Daniel's voice when he replied, "I closed the door on my past a long time ago. I would rather not reopen it."

And yet, when he had needed a name for a fictitious wife from Texas, he had chosen a name from that past. Maybe that door wasn't closed as tightly as he wanted her to believe.

Though they had been walking very slowly, they'd gone some distance from the resort buildings. B.J. could barely hear the strains of the music from the outdoor lounge. Daniel paused to look at the moonlight-frosted ocean. "It's nice out here, isn't it?"

Brushing a breeze-tossed strand of hair away from her eyes, B.J. nodded. "Very different from Dallas."

"Not quite as exotic as the places you've daydreamed about."

She let that comment go without a response. It was hard to define how she felt about being here. The beauty of the scenery was undeniable, as were the attractions of the luxury resort. Had she not been so constantly aware of those hidden watchers and so continuously worried about her inappropriate responses to Daniel, she could be enjoying her stay here much more than she might have expected, considering her initial response to the place.

He turned to face her, draping both arms over her shoulders and clasping his hands loosely behind her head. "I would like to know exactly how you found me, but perhaps we should concentrate on our roles again for a while. It would seem very odd if a doting husband didn't stop even once to kiss his wife during a romantic moonlight stroll."

She cleared her throat. "Maybe his wife is the sort who prefers to do her kissing in a less public place."

Smiling, he brushed his lips along her cheek. "Maybe she's so wrapped up in her husband that she doesn't even notice if anyone else is around."

As corny as that sounded, B.J. had little trouble believing it could be possible. Standing this close to Daniel, with his arms around her and his eyes locked with hers, she was having a hard time believing they weren't the only two people on the planet.

"A bit full of yourself, aren't you?" she managed to tease lightly.

He chuckled, his breath warm against her temple. "Just playing a part, darlin'."

He didn't have to keep reminding her of that, she assured herself. She wasn't likely to take his attentions seriously.

If there was one thing she didn't need, it was to fall in love with a self-admitted con man.

Daniel kissed her cheek again and then the corner of her mouth. And then his lips settled firmly on hers.

They were simply playing their parts, B.J. reminded herself as she slid her arms around Daniel's waist. Putting on an act, she thought as she tilted her head and parted her lips to cooperate with the kiss. Yet when he tightened his arms around her and deepened the kiss with a thrust of his tongue, she forgot about performing for any audience except him.

Regardless of his motivation, there was no doubt that Daniel Andreas was one hell of a kisser.

The initial embrace lasted for a long time, as did the kiss that followed. And the slow, deep, mesmerizing one after that. She was plastered against him now, and it was impossible not to notice that he was at least partially aroused.

Proving only that he was a man, she reminded herself when she finally drew her head back to end the kiss. No one could help responding to kisses like those.

She was very close to melting into a puddle in the sand herself.

Daniel's voice was rather hoarse when he said, "I think it's time to go in."

He caught her hand when she would have drawn out of touching distance. Reminded that the performance wasn't quite over for the evening, she slowed her steps and tried to appear besotted with him as they made their way back to their room.

The problem was, it was entirely too easy to pull that look off. And she was becoming increasingly concerned that—on her part, at least—it wasn't all an act.

Chapter Six

Three in the morning, and Daniel was lying in the dark in the suite's sitting room. Alone. B.J. had turned in soon after they'd returned from their walk, but he had told her he had some paperwork to look over first.

Even after he had procrastinated as long as possible with the paperwork and turned off the lights in the sitting room, he hadn't been able to make himself go into the bedroom. Instead he sprawled on the uncomfortable sofa, his sock-clad feet hanging over one end, eyes wide open as he stared at the ceiling.

After those kisses on the beach—kisses that had begun for the benefit of anyone who might be watching but had swiftly evolved into much more—he hadn't trusted himself to join B.J. in the bed.

He had told her there was a good chance they would be leaving tomorrow. In actuality, the odds were only about fifty-fifty that he could wrap his business up that quickly. Still, he was going to do everything he could to get this over with as quickly as possible.

Drake and his men were dangerous—but it was beginning to feel as though Brittany Jeanne Samples posed the real threat to the life Daniel had created for himself.

Too restless to wait in the suite for Daniel the next morning, B.J. donned a black two-piece bathing suit and a floral-on-black pareu, deciding it was time to try out the pool.

She hadn't actually seen Daniel since he had sent her off to bed alone the night before. She'd found a note from him when she'd woken. It lay on the pillow Daniel hadn't used last night.

"Darling," he had written neatly, "I'll be in meetings most of the morning. I hope you'll be able to entertain yourself until I rejoin you."

She suspected that it was as much mischief as role-playing that had made him add, "I'll carry the memory of last night with me until I have you in my arms again. Your Daniel."

Oh, puhleeze, she had thought with a roll of her eyes. Was Daniel's idea of marital bliss really so smarmy or was this his attempt at a private joke?

Either way, she had tucked his note into her tote bag rather than tossing it into the trash, and she didn't want to spend much time examining her motives for hanging on to it.

It was while she was stashing the note away that she realized both her cell phone and her wallet were missing from the bag. Since B.J. had arrived at the resort, she hadn't needed them—so there was no telling how long they had been gone. Everything else was still in place, but no amount of digging through her usual clutter produced either of those items.

It occurred to her that there was now nothing in the bag to indicate that she was anyone other than who she had said. Daniel's wife. Anyone snooping through her things might wonder at the absence of a wallet, but they wouldn't find anything to disprove her cover story.

Maybe she should have considered that someone from outside had been through her bag already and had taken her possessions. But for some reason she had no doubt that Daniel was the pilferer. He had been so thorough in making sure she went along with this charade; he wouldn't neglect hiding any evidence that they were pulling off a scam.

Knowing she would be wasting her time searching the suite for her things, she picked up her paperback and headed out of the suite.

Even knowing Drake had designed it himself, she couldn't help but admire the pool. It was so beautiful, with its surrounding tropical plants, the natural-looking waterfalls, the curving lines of the pool itself.

She selected an umbrella-shaded poolside chair, ordered a glass of orange juice from a server who seemed

to appear out of nowhere, then leaned back and opened
the book she had purchased yesterday. Fifteen minutes
later she closed it again. She was too restless to read.
Her body ached for…something. It seemed safest to define it as exercise.

She slipped into the pool, which was still unoccupied
this early in the morning. The pleasantly warm water
closed around her like a lover's arms. Because the anal-
ogy made that vague ache inside her intensify, she
began to swim, counting laps until she couldn't complete another one.

She most definitely burned off energy during her
vigorous swim, but nothing else had changed. Her mind
was still filled with thoughts of Daniel as she boosted
herself out of the pool.

Water streaming off her, she reached for the towel
she had left beside the pool. She swiped the towel over
her hair and face and turned toward her chair—then
stopped.

A man sat in the chair next to the one in which she
had been trying to read earlier. He was young—probably close to her own age—and sandy-haired, with
friendly blue eyes and a pleasant smile. The skin on his
nose was peeling from a sunburn, and his cheeks were
unnaturally pink.

He couldn't look more innocent, but still she wondered if he was yet another employee of Drake's. Had
he been watching her for a reason?

"Good morning," she said evenly, reaching for her
pareu.

"Got yourself a workout this morning, didn't you?"

"I suppose so." She wrapped the fabric around her and knotted it at her left hip.

"I just came from a run on the beach," he confided. "I'm a morning person myself. But my wife, well, she doesn't think any vacation day really begins before noon. Sleeping in is a rare treat for her."

Something about the way he had said "my wife" made her smile and sink into her chair. "Honeymoon?"

"Yeah. How could you tell?"

She shrugged. "Newlywed vibes."

He laughed sheepishly. "My wife—um, Natalie— says I'm a compulsive talker. If you would rather be alone—"

"No. I was just out here killing time while my, er, husband is in a meeting."

"Are you on your honeymoon, too?"

"No, we've been married for a couple of years," she said, automatically falling back on the details Daniel had drilled into her. "We're combining a vacation with a business trip."

"Great place, isn't it? They've been treating us like royalty. Maybe you're used to that sort of thing? For Natalie and me it's a real novelty. We saved for more than a year for this honeymoon."

B.J. wanted to tell him that it was new for her, too, but that wouldn't have fit the background Daniel had created for her. "It is a lovely resort."

"My name is Kurt, by the way. Kurt McGuire. We're from Tulsa."

"I'm B.J. Sam—um, Andreas. From Dallas."

"Yeah? Neighboring states. Makes us sort of neigh-bors, too, I guess."

There was some distance between Dallas and Tulsa, but if he wanted to claim her as a neighbor, what the heck. "Sure."

"I'm an attorney—well, I just passed the bar, but I've got a job lined up in my uncle's firm. My wife's a third-year medical student, which is why we only get five days for a honeymoon, because she has to do rota-tions this summer. What do you and your husband do?"

The guy certainly was a talker. She wondered cyni-cally how long it would take the practice of law to drain the open friendliness right out of him.

It suddenly occurred to her that Daniel hadn't actu-ally told her what his job was supposed to be. "My hus-band is in investments," she hazarded. "I keep myself busy with volunteer work," she added, dutifully—if re-luctantly—staying in character.

"Do you have any children?"

This was her cue to look sad, she remembered. Oddly enough, as her mind filled with images of little dark-haired, dark-eyed replicas of Daniel, it wasn't that hard to pull it off. "No, we haven't been so fortunate yet."

Perhaps she was a better actress than she had thought. Kurt reached out to pat her bare knee. The gesture was more brotherly than presumptuous. "I'm sure everything will work out for you."

She couldn't help smiling in response to his earnest

expression. He seemed like a genuinely nice man. "Thank you. And by the way, congratulations on your marriage and on passing the bar."

Someone cleared his throat rather forcefully behind them. Both B.J. and Kurt looked around to find Daniel approaching them, his dark brows drawn downward between hard obsidian eyes.

B.J. had thought before that there were times when Daniel could look rather dangerous. This was one of those times.

Kurt quickly pulled his hand back to his own knee. "I have a feeling that this is your husband."

"Yes, it is." B.J. smiled at Daniel, pushing inconvenient memories of last night's kisses to the back of her mind. "Daniel, this is my new friend, Kurt McGuire. Kurt, my husband, Daniel Andreas."

Daniel swept the other man with a hard look that traveled slowly from sunburned cheeks to the hand that had just rested on B.J.'s knee. A slight nod was the only greeting he offered.

Kurt cleared his throat and stood. "Nice to meet you, Daniel. I was just, uh—"

"Patting my wife's leg?" Daniel supplied silkily when Kurt faltered for a moment.

"Daniel." B.J. gave him a warning look as she stood.

"You know, I bet *my* wife is awake now. I'd better go see if she's ready for breakfast." Giving B.J. a quick, careful smile, Kurt hurried away.

Planting her hands on her hips, B.J. stared at Daniel. "That was incredibly rude."

"The guy needs a lesson in keeping his hands to himself."

"And you think it's your place to give him that lesson?"

"If I find his hand on your leg again, you're damned straight I'll give him that lesson."

She made a choked sound of sheer disbelief. "Might I remind you that we are not really—"

"I know you were just being friendly to the guy," Daniel interrupted quickly, giving her a look of warning. "He's the one I don't trust, not you."

"He's a nice, chatty man on his honeymoon who was simply waiting for his bride to wake up. And you were very rude to him."

She turned to snatch up her book from the chair, intending to stalk back to their suite. Daniel caught her arm and turned her around to face him. "You're probably right. I really shouldn't blame the guy for being drawn to you. The way you look this morning, he probably couldn't help himself."

B.J. rolled her eyes. Since her dripping hair was still plastered against her head, she wore no makeup and the modest black bikini only emphasized her lack of curves, she found it hard to take his outrageous flattery serious.

"Yes, well, surprisingly enough, I think it was more boredom than uncontrollable lust for my extraordinary body that made a newlywed man so friendly. So—are you through with your meetings today?"

He hesitated a moment—as if he would have liked to argue more about her conversation with Kurt—but then he shook his head. "No, I have to go back in. I just wanted to tell you that Drake urges you to feel free to make use of the spa or salons this morning. I can't join you for lunch, but Drake has arranged for you and me to have a picnic dinner on an island he owns offshore. He says it's a beautiful spot, and only the most privileged of his guests are invited to make use of it."

"I, um—" She glanced around to make sure no one was nearby, then lowered her voice to little more than a whisper. "I thought we were leaving today?"

"I said there's a chance we'd be able to leave today," he reminded her. "It's looking doubtful now. In the meantime, we're still playing along. So I'll meet you at the marina at five o'clock."

It wasn't a question. He expected her to meet him. Since she had agreed to cooperate, she merely nodded. "I'll be there."

Hands on her shoulders, he pulled her toward him and planted a long, hard kiss on her lips.

"I'll see you at five," he said when he finally released her.

He walked away before she could recover her voice sufficiently to answer him.

Staring after him, she ran her fingertips slowly across her still-tingling lips. If she hadn't known better, she would have almost believed Daniel really had been jealous.

Had he not chosen a life of crime—or whatever it was he was involved with—Daniel could have had an impressive career as an actor.

* * *

Almost an hour after he'd left B.J. at the pool, Daniel could still picture her sitting in that chair, smiling at the man with his hand on her bare, damp knee. She had obviously just come out of the pool. Droplets of water had glistened on her skin, and her face was still rosy from exertion. She had looked young, fresh, natural. Desirable.

Knowing that B.J.'s confidence was rather shaky when it came to her own sex appeal, he wasn't surprised that she hadn't even suspected Kurt McGuire was coming on to her. Maybe she'd been right that time—though even a blissful newlywed had probably noticed just how good B.J. had looked in that black bathing suit that had fit her slender figure like a cat's fur.

He had certainly noticed, Daniel thought with a scowl. Seeing her looking like that and smiling cozily at another man had hit him like a blow directly to the chest.

It was the first time in his adult life that Daniel had been struck by a full-blown case of totally male possessiveness. Not to mention sheer jealousy at having B.J. smiling at anyone but himself.

"Daniel?" Drake spoke rather curtly from the table behind him. "You still with us?"

The question had several meanings, but Daniel answered only the most obvious one when he turned and nodded. "Yeah. Just admiring the scenery."

"You'll have time for that later. Let's stick to business now, all right?"

Good suggestion. Daniel needed to stick to business when it came to B.J., too.

On her own for lunch, B.J. considered ordering room service. But it was such a beautiful day—and the truth was, she was tired of sitting in the suite by herself.

She went to the outdoor café instead, finding a cozy table with a beautiful ocean view. A solicitous waiter took her order for a salad made of mixed greens and grilled salmon, which was delivered to her very quickly, accompanied by whole-grain bread with whipped honey-butter spread.

Sipping iced mint tea, she told herself that she could enjoy this lovely meal without missing Daniel one bit. It wasn't as if she had grown so quickly accustomed to his company, she assured herself. They'd only been to-gether a couple of days, and their interactions had been more for the benefit of others than for themselves.

She really didn't even know him now, since he'd been playing a part—even with her—ever since she'd found him in Missouri. After tomorrow she doubted that she would ever see him again, since he had shown lit-tle interest in revisiting his past.

Which didn't mean she wouldn't think of him. Often. Unfortunately he fascinated her as much now as he ever had.

"Good afternoon, Brittany."

She glanced up from her salad with a frown in re-sponse to the name. "It's B.J.," she said automatically, only then identifying the speaker. "Hello, Ingrid."

"B.J." The blonde motioned toward the empty chair at the other side of the table. "Are you expecting someone?"

"No. My husband is in meetings until this afternoon. Would you like to join me?"

Looking pleased, Ingrid nodded and eagerly pulled out the other chair. "Guess what I've been doing this morning."

Though B.J. was surprised by the other woman's chatty manner, she played along. "Practicing your singing?"

"Yes. The band in the lounge helped me work up a set—three songs. I'm going back to practice again after their lunch break, just to make sure everything will be perfect tonight."

"I'm sure you'll be wonderful," B.J. said, though she was sure of no such thing. For all she knew, Ingrid had a voice like a frog.

Drake certainly hadn't seemed enthused about giving her a gig in the lounge, but that could well have nothing to do with her talent. More likely, he preferred his women to stay quietly by his side, looking pretty and warming his bed without drawing too much attention to themselves.

"I'm a little nervous," Ingrid confided, accepting a glass of iced mint tea from a server with a smile of thanks.

"That's understandable. Aren't you going to order lunch?"

Though she looked a bit wistfully at the basket of

bread, Ingrid shook her head. "I never eat before I perform. I just came here for a glass of tea."

She didn't look as though she ate much, period. B.J. was naturally slim herself, but she could tell when a woman stayed thin by depriving herself as Ingrid, with her natural curves, apparently did.

Giving the bread basket a little push, she said casually, "At least have a little bread. You need something to give you the energy for a dynamite performance tonight."

"Maybe just a bite." Ingrid plucked a slice from the well-filled basket and then, apparently deciding it wouldn't hurt to embellish it a bit, spread a thin layer of honey butter on top.

Watching in satisfaction, B.J. distracted her by asking, "You said you're nervous about your performance tonight. Is this your first time to perform in public?"

"Oh, no. I've been in lots of beauty pageants, and singing was always my talent. I was first runner-up in the Miss Minnesota pageant two years ago. I should have won, but the winner founded some sort of charity for underprivileged kids and the judges made a big deal out of her, like she was Mother Teresa or somebody.

"Anyway," she added, shaking off a scowl, "I'm nervous because it's been a while since I've sung with a real band and everything. And I know Judson didn't really want me to sing here, so I want to do an especially good job and make him realize he was wrong about my talent."

"Have you and Mr. Drake been seeing each other long?"

"Oh, we aren't really seeing each other, if you know what I mean. We met at a big party a few months ago, and I've been sort of staying with him since.

"He told me he would help me with my career," she added with a renewed flash of bitterness. "So far all he's done is line up a couple of modeling gigs to keep me busy when he's off traveling. Probably has other women everywhere he goes—and he probably makes big promises to them, too."

B.J. noted that Ingrid seemed more annoyed by the lack of career opportunities than the fact that Drake was seeing other women. "Have another slice of bread."

Ingrid took another slice without seeming to notice what she was doing. "Your husband is really good-looking. Nice, too. He's always been real polite to me, without ever getting weird about it, you know?"

Since B.J. couldn't say the same about Drake, she merely smiled.

"How long have you been married?"

"Two years."

"No kids?"

"No." B.J. made an effort to look sad again. "I had a miscarriage last fall. We're still trying, but no luck yet."

"Oh. Sorry."

"It's okay." B.J. was particularly uncomfortable with this part of the story she had been instructed to give.

"I'm sure you'll have a kid soon," Ingrid offered encouragingly. "And I bet it's fun trying, right? After all, you're married to a hunk, and he's obviously crazy about you."

Rather amused by Ingrid's awkward effort to make her feel better—something the other woman obviously didn't have much experience with—B.J. smiled. "He is a hunk, isn't he?"

Looking relieved that the possibility of an emotional scene had passed, Ingrid nodded eagerly. "He's gorgeous. Judson's good-looking and all, but if Daniel wasn't married, let me tell you—I'd make a play for him in a minute. A couple of the other girls already have, because a gold ring doesn't mean squat to them unless they're wearing it. But Daniel, he keeps them all at a distance. I could see why when I watched the two of you together last night. You're, like, a perfect couple."

"You, um, think so?"

"Oh, yeah. I mean, I'm not ready to settle down and have kids myself—I really want to have a fabulous singing career first—but if I was, I'd want something like you've got with Daniel. He's good-looking and rich and powerful and he treats you like a queen. Every woman's dream, right?"

"I…I suppose so." Being treated like a queen had never been B.J.'s dream, but she supposed the wife Daniel had created for this fantasy would like that sort of thing.

Ingrid looked in both directions before leaning slightly toward B.J. and saying in a low voice, "I guess it doesn't bother you too bad that Daniel's mixed up with Judson, huh? I mean, I know they're going to make a lot of money, but I just hope it doesn't all go sour on them."

And just what the hell was she supposed to say in response to that? "I, um—"

"I know, I know. We're not supposed to talk about the men's business. Judson's made that real clear, and I guess your Daniel has, too. But, jeez, you can't hang around them very long without figuring out they're up to something shady. I even heard Daniel tell Judson that they've got to be real careful the feds don't catch on to whatever they're scheming before the big payoff comes through. Doesn't it make you mad when they act like we're too stupid to figure things out?"

"Yes," B.J. said slowly, setting down her fork and folding her hands on the table. She had suddenly lost her appetite. "Yes, it does."

"Oh, well, I guess everything will work out. Judson said he's never been caught at anything yet and neither has your Daniel. Neither of them are Boy Scouts, but I never was interested in Boy Scouts anyway, you know? I like men with money and power."

She patted the diamond pendant hanging around her neck, then reached out to touch the bracelet on B.J.'s wrist. "You know what I mean, right? I just wish Judson would use some of that influence to help me get a recording contract."

B.J. sipped her iced tea to avoid having to respond, since she wouldn't have had a clue what to say anyway.

Ingrid's face lit up. "Hey, I have an idea."

B.J. couldn't help thinking rather cattily that it must be

a novel experience for her, but then she told herself to stop being snide. Ingrid was obviously trying to be friendly.

It was likely that she didn't have a lot of experience making friends with other women. Yet B.J. had defended her last night, cornering Drake into giving Ingrid a chance to sing, and that might have been something Ingrid wasn't accustomed to coming from another woman.

"What's your idea?" She was almost afraid to ask.

"Why don't you come listen to me practice after lunch? You can tell me how I sound."

"Oh, I don't know much about music. I—"

"Please," Ingrid said quietly. "I'd feel better if someone gave me an honest opinion. No one who works for Judson would dare say anything negative. I think you'll be honest.

"And besides," she added with a smile, "you're from Texas. You know country music."

B.J. didn't have the heart to refuse, even though she actually preferred rock to country. It wasn't as if she had anything better to do, anyway. "I can come for a little while," she agreed. "I have to go back to my suite at three or so to get ready to meet Daniel, but I'm open until then."

"Great." Ingrid was so pleased, she reached for another slice of bread.

Chapter Seven

As Daniel had instructed—or to be more precise, as he had ordered—B.J. appeared at the marina at exactly five o'clock. She had considered being ten or fifteen minutes late, just to make a statement, but then decided that would be petty and childish.

She was above that sort of thing, she assured herself loftily. But if Daniel got all bossy and snappy with her again, she was going to chew off a large piece of his hide, to use an old Texas expression.

She had changed into red capri pants and a sleeveless white cotton shirt with red piping at the armholes and V neckline. A thin red cardigan was knotted loosely around her shoulders, in case the temperature dropped as the late-May evening advanced. Red-and-white-checked flip-flops completed the look, so that she was gazing at a coordinated stranger in the mirror again when she finished dressing.

Sunglasses and her paperback—both for when the sun was still out—were the only other things she packed into her canvas tote, since she didn't know what else she might need for this picnic outing. Especially since willpower wasn't something she could stuff into a bag, she thought ruefully, once again remembering last night's kisses on the beach.

She was dismayed to see Bernard waiting at the boat slip with Daniel. Was she going to be forced to endure a picnic with Bernard? If so, she could feel an imaginary migraine coming on, which she would use as an excuse to cut the outing short. Actually, after spending any time at all with Bernard, she doubted she would have to fake a headache.

Bernard was dressed in his usual uniform. Jeans, a blue T-shirt and a loose white linen jacket that made him look a bit like a refrigerator. Even though the look was twenty years out of style, the white jacket did a decent job of hiding the shoulder holster he undoubtedly wore beneath it. The sleeves were pushed up as a concession to the warmth of the afternoon, but she doubted he would remove the jacket within sight of any of the guests.

Having changed at some point during the afternoon into a loose white shirt and khaki slacks with espadrilles, Daniel stepped forward to greet her with a smile and an outstretched hand. "Punctual, as always," he said, brushing a kiss against her cheek.

She merely gave him a look. Maybe he had forgotten that little scene beside the pool earlier, but she wanted him to know that she had not.

"Afternoon, Mrs. Andreas."

She nodded. "Bernard."

"Mr. Drake went all out to make sure you'll have a nice picnic. Chef's packed a real special meal for you."

"How thoughtful." B.J. allowed Daniel to help her onto the sleek cruiser, where she settled on a deep-cushioned seat. Daniel sat beside her, and Bernard took the controls, nodding to a brown-skinned teenager who stood by to assist them in casting off.

The cruise took half an hour, and B.J. had to admit the time passed pleasantly. Daniel stretched his long legs out comfortably, one of his arms slung casually behind her. She enjoyed being on the water. Unconcerned about her tossing hair, she held on to her sunglasses and turned her face into the brisk, salty breeze.

The island was as pretty as a calendar page. Bernard docked the boat at a pier marked with bold signs marked Private Property: No Trespassing.

Beyond a stretch of clean, inviting beach, a picnic pavilion had been nestled into the landscaping. Covered by a picturesque thatched roof, the shelter had three open sides that could be closed off from weather by roll-down awnings. Kitchen facilities had been built into the back wall—an enormous grill, a sink and preparation and serving counters, beneath which were cabinets presumably holding supplies. Two doors marked with male and female silhouettes indicated restrooms at either end of the wall.

The stone floor looked recently swept, so apparently the pavilion received regular maintenance, perhaps daily. Two large teak picnic tables and several teak lounge chairs provided seating for more than a dozen people. Tiki torches surrounded the shelter to provide illumination for evening parties, and party lights were strung inside the pavilion ceiling.

"There's electricity?" B.J. asked in surprise.

"By way of large generators, back behind the shelter," Bernard explained. "They aren't on right now, since you and Mr. Andreas won't be needing electricity for your picnic. The restrooms have skylights that will provide all the illumination you need for daytime use."

Setting an enormous hamper on one of the tables, he then handed Daniel a key on a large yellow holder. "This opens all the cabinets and the restroom doors. We keep them locked because sometimes trespassers make use of the island despite the signs, but we send patrols out enough to keep it from being a big problem. You'll find seat cushions and anything else you might need in the cabinets. Make yourselves comfortable while you're here."

Daniel set a covered plastic box of picnic supplies on the table next to the hamper. "Will you be joining us for dinner?"

B.J. was relieved when Bernard shook his bald head.

"I'll be back to collect you later. Mr. Drake wants you to have a relaxing meal—just the two of you."

B.J. was relieved that Bernard was leaving, but the thought of being alone on Drake's island with Daniel didn't make her overly comfortable, either. Especially after the kisses they had shared the last time they were alone on a beach together.

Watching the cruiser disappear into the distance, B.J. turned back to Daniel with a forced smile. "How do you suppose Drake ended up with this island?"

Daniel shrugged. "Who knows? He claimed he often hosts parties here for celebrities wanting to get away from the paparazzi. Other times—like today—he has guests come over just to spend a day relaxing and enjoying a few hours away from cell phones and computers. During the height of tourist season, he said the island is reserved nearly every day. It's even a popular wedding site."

Looking around at the trees and birds and flowers and beach, B.J. had no doubt that Drake's island had a steady stream of visitors who longed to get away from ringing phones and beeping computers.

Because that subject seemed to have been exhausted, she moved toward the picnic hamper. "Let's see what's in this thing. I'm starving."

Daniel chuckled, though she thought he sounded distracted. "You're always hungry."

"Pretty much. I'm lucky I have the Walker metabolism. The Samples family tend to be somewhat stockier. My brother takes after that side. There's no fat on him because he's totally into sports and running, but he's more broad-shouldered and squarely built than the Walkers." Not that Daniel cared about any of this information, of course. She was just babbling nervously.

Yet he proved that he had been paying attention by asking, "And what about your sister? Seems like I remember her being pretty slender."

"Dawne has the kind of figure that makes men walk into walls," B.J. replied matter-of-factly. "I guess she got the best of the Walkers and the Samples."

"As did you."

She hadn't been fishing for a compliment. Opening the picnic hamper, she began to dig busily inside, changing the subject again. "Wow. This thing is packed."

Daniel had been standing rather stiffly, staring at the water in the direction in which Bernard had disappeared. He seemed to give himself a mental shake and turned then to assist her. "Hang on. I'll get the seat cushions out of the storage cabinets."

She watched as he placed brightly colored cushions on the picnic benches and lounge chairs. A bit more digging produced a pile of straw mats, two of which Daniel arranged at opposite sides of the table.

Having watched him with a frown, B.J. asked, "Daniel, what's wrong? You've been acting oddly ever since Bernard left."

"Sorry. Guess I'm just distracted."

"You aren't still angry that I talked with Kurt earlier,

are you?" Because if he was, she intended to make it clear that—

But Daniel was shaking his head, answering in a firm voice, "I was never angry about that. I just want you to be careful who you talk to while you're here, that's all. You never know who's working with Drake."

There was still something off in his expression. Cocking her head, B.J. studied his face. "How did your meetings go today?"

He shrugged ruefully. "Not well."

So that explained it. She reached into the insulated, ice-pack-lined hamper and began to pull out covered dishes, thinking maybe he would open up more during the meal. Maybe he would finally tell her more about what he was involved with now that they were completely alone.

"This," she said a few minutes later, "is not what I would call a picnic. I don't think I've ever had such fancy food from a picnic basket."

Perhaps remembering that B.J. enjoyed seafood, Drake had provided a virtual feast for them. Cold cracked crab, huge prawns marinated with lemon and spices, potato salad niçoise, marinated asparagus spears. An assortment of cheeses and crackers and thinly sliced cold meats, with fresh fruits and delicate pastries for dessert. Nothing chocolate, she noted with a sigh.

Daniel looked up from his plate—a real china plate rather than the paper plates that made up her typical picnics back in Texas. "Drake takes great pleasure in showing off. This spread is meant to demonstrate for us that he is accustomed to the best of everything—for himself *and* his guests."

"So where did he get his money?" B.J. asked, though she doubted she would get a straight answer. "Did he inherit it?"

"Hardly. Judson Drake is what you would call a self-made man. Including his name, by the way."

"I had already guessed that. There's nothing about the guy that rings true to me."

Daniel shrugged and popped a bite of crab into his mouth. "Yes, well…"

She glared across the table at him. "I'm fully aware that he's not the only one creating an entire persona out of thin air."

Daniel smiled and lifted his glass to her before taking a sip of the expensive wine Drake had provided with the meal.

She shook her head in bemusement. "This whole situation is just bizarre."

"You have no idea how much," Daniel muttered, draining his glass.

"Tell me what you've done since I left the ranch," Daniel urged a few moments later, resting his forearms on the table to study her face. "Did you go to college? Have you always worked for your uncles?"

She didn't even pretend to herself that he was all that interested in her life. More likely, he was trying to keep her talking about herself as a means of preventing further questions about him. But since she knew how stubborn he could be about not answering anything he didn't want to answer, she figured she might as well let him lead the conversation. For now, anyway.

"I went to college. The University of Texas. I majored in accounting—like my father and my brother."

"You didn't care for accounting?"

"No. I worked in my father's office for a year, then had to quit before I went slowly insane. So I tried retail, working in a department store. That lasted six months. Since then I've worked in various computer-oriented jobs, and went to work for my uncles just over a year ago. Supposedly they were going to train me in the business, but mostly they've taken advantage of my computer skills. Tracking you down was the first field assignment they've given me."

Daniel looked somewhat stunned. "You found me that easily and it was your first assignment?"

"I didn't say it was easy," she corrected, though she took some satisfaction from the chagrined look in his eyes. "I was about to give up when I stumbled across someone who thought he had seen you with Drake and directed me toward the farmhouse."

"Who? And what led you to St. Louis in the first place? That isn't where I live."

"I know. You move around a lot. Three weeks ago, you sent your aunt Maria a birthday card postmarked St. Louis. She showed it to me. She also gave me a snapshot of you. If you looked through my wallet when you lifted it, you must have seen the photograph. She said she took it herself last time you visited her—about three years ago."

"I didn't rifle through your belongings," he said a bit defensively. "I simply put them away for safekeeping. And you went to see my aunt?"

"Yes. She's your only living relative, so I thought you might contact her occasionally. It seems you do more than that. She told me you've been sending her money in increasing amounts every month since you left her home when you turned eighteen."

Daniel looked uncomfortable. "I've tried to help her out a little."

"According to her, it's been more than a little. She told me that if it hadn't been for you, she'd have ended up in a state-run home a long time ago."

Scowling now, Daniel wadded up his linen napkin and tossed it onto the table. "Sounds like you had quite a chat with her."

And he didn't like it....

"I wasn't trying to pump her for information. If you'll remember, my only objective was to invite you to a party. She said you were in St. Louis. I tracked down the zip code, showed your picture at every hotel in that area and I had just about given up when someone mentioned having seen you with Drake. One tip led to another and now here we are."

"Here we are," Daniel repeated in a mutter. "It's a miracle you didn't set off all kinds of alarms within Drake's circles. Apparently you never wandered onto his radar screen during your search."

"You were lucky, I guess. And lucky that Bernard immediately assumed I was your wife and didn't ask a lot of questions."

"And lucky that you kept your head and didn't blow everything by blurting out that I wasn't your husband."

"You didn't give me much chance to do so. I don't think I've ever seen anyone move as quickly as you did when you recognized me."

Daniel smiled wryly. "When your life is at stake, you don't waste a lot of time considering options."

B.J. selected a cherry tart from the assortment of pastries. "Your aunt is very fond of you. And proud of you. She told me you're a very successful businessman. She didn't know what type of business you're in, but she thinks it has something to do with computers."

Looking out toward the water, Daniel continued to scowl.

B.J. swallowed the last bite of the tart and reached for her wineglass. "It really bothers you that I went to see her, doesn't it?"

"It bothers me that you tracked her down so easily—and me," he admitted. "Perhaps I was being arrogant in thinking she would be safe even if Drake figured out that the background I gave him was phony."

"There was no reason for you to worry about her. Her last name is different from yours—either of yours. There's nothing at all to connect her with you."

"And yet you did."

"I had the old records from the ranch," she reminded

him. "Molly got hold of them and found your aunt's name and number as your next of kin."

"An invitation to a party hardly seems justification for a wholesale invasion of my privacy."

"You're absolutely right."

He seemed surprised that she had conceded so quickly, and without any effort to defend her actions.

"I'm sorry," she added. "I didn't consider the possibility that you would have good reasons for not wanting to be found. I was focusing on proving myself to my uncles, and Molly is sort of obsessed with her plans for her parents' surprise party. Neither of us gave enough thought to your right to be left alone. We thought you'd want to be included in the party. It certainly never occurred to me—to either of us—that finding you could actually put your life in danger."

"You had no way of knowing that, of course," he acknowledged.

"That's no excuse. We should have realized that if you wanted to maintain a connection with our family, you'd have at least called once during the past dozen years."

He looked at her then. "Did you think about me after I left?"

This time she was the one who glanced away. "Of course I did. I considered you a friend."

More than a friend, of course. She'd had a desperate crush on him—but there was no need to mention that just now.

"I thought of you sometimes, as well," he murmured.

"I remembered the way you always told me I didn't have to be trapped in my past. That I could do anything I wanted with my future."

"I'm sure several people told you that. I know Uncle Jared and Aunt Cassie must have."

"They did," he admitted. "But when you said it, for some reason, I believed it."

B.J. toyed with the napkin in her lap, pleating the fabric tightly. "I was just a kid. I'm surprised you took anything I said seriously."

"I took everything you said seriously."

"So what happened after you left? How did you get from there to…here?"

For just a few moments, he had been open to her. Now suddenly he was closed off again. "I told you I was going to make something of myself."

"And what have you become?"

After only a brief hesitation he replied offhandedly, "A prosperous man. Or at least, I'm headed that way."

She continued to look steadily at him, searching his expression for meanings behind the words. "Having a lot of money is your idea of amounting to something?"

"Of course. Maybe money can't buy happiness, but it can sure provide everything a man needs to keep himself comfortable during the pursuit."

"Funny. It was just two days ago that you cautioned me not to confuse wealth with character and class."

A little muscle flickered at the corner of his eye. "I said that?"

"You did. You were trying to set me at ease when I

said I felt out of place among all the rich people at the resort."

"Yes, well, I never said *I* felt out of place there. Or that I was someone who wanted to be admired for my character, as I'm sure you do. Living in luxury, having anything I want with a quick phone call—that's who I aspire to be."

"You are so full of crap."

Her cross comment startled a quizzical laugh out of him. "I beg your pardon?"

"I don't know why you're here exactly, but I think there's a lot more to it than simple greed. Maybe you want the money to take care of your aunt. Maybe you hate Drake for some reason and want to take him down. Or maybe you just enjoy the challenge of out-conning a con man. But it isn't just the desire for wealth that motivates you."

He seemed momentarily disconcerted, but then he reached for the wine bottle, breaking the visual contact between them. "Would you like some more of this?"

"No, thank you." She stood and moved out of the shelter, walking slowly down to the beach. Shells and driftwood were scattered on the sand, begging to be explored. She carried a few crackers with her, tossing them to hovering, squawking seagulls.

She laughed when they grew bold enough to practically snatch the bites from her fingertips. "Shameless beggars."

"Remember the day we fed the Canada geese that lived in the ponds on your uncle's ranch? The geese were so aggressive, they almost knocked us to our knees to take the bread from our hands."

She hadn't realized Daniel had moved to stand behind her until he spoke. "I remember," she said, turning to face him. "We laughed so hard I got hiccups."

"It was the first time I had laughed like that in months," he murmured. "Since the day I found my mother, actually."

It was also the day he had cried. She could still remember the moment his laughter had turned to tears. He had been appalled by the dampness on his cheeks, perhaps expecting her to react with discomfort. Or worse, pity.

Instead she had somehow instinctively understood that he had needed to release the emotions locked inside him for so long. Emotions that had been triggered by their laughter. And even though she had been very young, only fourteen, she had held his hand and told him matter-of-factly that she understood the need to cry sometimes. She did so herself every once in a while—and she hadn't been through nearly what Daniel had.

He hadn't shed more than a few tears. He had wiped them away with the backs of his hands, leaving dirty streaks on his brown cheeks. Without his asking, she had assured him that no one would ever hear from her that he wasn't quite as tough as he wanted everyone to believe.

He had caught her arm when she'd started to turn away from him. The kiss he had given her then had been brief, awkward, unexpected. She had suspected ever since that it had been intended as a distraction of sorts.

He had wanted to leave her with the memory of her first kiss rather than his momentary weakness.

She remembered both. Vividly.

Dusting cracker crumbs off her hands, she turned to face him now. "Is the money really so important to you? It's not really too late to walk away from this, is it?"

"My business here is very important to me," he answered curtly. "And it's much too late to walk away. I'm only sorry you got tangled up in it."

Her throat was tight when she turned away again. "So am I."

Chapter Eight

Tearing his gaze away from B.J., who sat in one of the teak lounge chairs with the paperback she had pulled out of her tote bag, Daniel glanced at his watch for the dozenth time in the past hour.

It was just after seven o'clock. Bernard should have returned for them by now.

He glanced at B.J. again. Even though there was still enough light to see the pages, she was looking at the book so fiercely that he suspected she was having to work hard to concentrate on her reading. She hadn't said much of anything to him since their talk on the beach, when she had told him she was sorry she'd gotten mixed up with him.

That had stung a little, though he didn't blame her at all for feeling that way.

She was making him remember things he had tried very hard to forget. Making him regret choices he had made during the years that had passed since that innocent kiss at the Walker ranch. And that was really starting to tick him off.

Maybe it was just the silence between them that was getting to him now. It wasn't normal for B.J. to be so quiet for so long. Combined with Bernard's tardiness— and the odd feeling he'd had ever since Bernard left them there—B.J.'s pouting was making him cranky.

She was annoyed because he wouldn't tell her more about his dealings with Drake. He knew it wouldn't appease her to tell her that he was trying to protect her by involving her as little as possible.

He sat in the lounge chair beside her. "Good book?"

Holding her place with one finger, she closed the covers. "Not bad."

"Would you like a snack or something? There were cookies and pastries left over, you know."

"I'm not hungry right now, thanks."

"A miracle in itself."

She gave a perfunctory smile in response to his teasing, then glanced toward the water. "When is Bernard supposed to return?"

Was she so bored with his company that she was even looking forward to seeing Bernard again? "Anytime now."

"I guess leaving the resort today is definitely out."

"I'm afraid so."

Another night in the suite with her. He wondered impassively if he would survive it with his sanity intact. Last night had been hard enough, knowing that she was sleeping so close.

He was clinging to his willpower by his fingertips where B.J. was concerned, but he had no intention of letting go. His memories of her were too special to risk hurting her now. And he *would* hurt her if he allowed her to start romanticizing him or the attraction between them. No matter what justification she tried to attribute to his actions, he was not a man for her to admire.

The problem was, when she looked at him now, she still saw the boy he used to be. And when she treated him that way, it was unexpectedly tempting to pretend that he hadn't long ago changed into someone she probably wouldn't like very much at all.

"I hope Bernard doesn't take much longer."

"Had enough of my company?" he asked lightly.

"It's just that I promised Ingrid we would catch her show in the lounge tonight."

His eyebrows rose. "You promised that at dinner last night?"

"No. I had lunch with her today and afterward I sat in on her rehearsal session with the lounge band."

He was genuinely surprised, since his few encounters with the cool, beautiful Ingrid had made him doubt that she had much interest in befriending other women. "How did that come about?"

B.J. shrugged. "We ended up in the same place at the

same time for lunch. One thing led to another. She wanted a friendly face at her rehearsal, since Creepy Guy has done such a good job of sabotaging her self-confidence."

"How was she?"

"She's not bad, actually. With a little training, and if someone advises her not to try so hard to emulate other singers' styles, she could be quite good."

"Good enough for a recording contract?"

"I don't know," she admitted. "I'm no expert on that sort of thing. But I think she has as much talent as several of the singers who've had moderately successful careers. And she certainly has the looks."

"So you actually like her?"

He watched as her nose wrinkled just a little. Just enough to make his mouth go dry. "I don't *dislike* her," she explained earnestly. "I just don't have much in common with her."

"No kidding."

"So maybe she's a bit…avaricious. She still deserves better than Creepy Guy and the insultingly condescending way he treats her. I hope she does make good in music so she can get away from him."

"Don't kid yourself, B.J. Ingrid is with Drake because she wants to be, not because she has to be. Whatever she might feel about him personally, she likes the perks that come with sleeping with him. But if it makes you feel any better, she's history after this weekend. Drake has hinted to me that he's become bored with her."

B.J. frowned, and he added, "I'm sure he plans to give her a generous parting gift. That's his usual style."

"At least she'll have the chance to perform tonight. Maybe that will lead to something better for her."

Daniel glanced at his watch again. "What time does she go on?"

"Nine o'clock. I'd feel bad if we had to miss it, since I promised her I'd be there."

He found her loyalty to a woman she'd only just met and didn't even particularly like rather touching—and typical of her. He hoped B.J.'s innate faith in other people—himself, for example—didn't get her heart broken someday.

"We should have time to change and make it to the lounge to hear her. If Bernard gets here soon," he added with another glance at the water.

"It seems odd that he'd be late, considering how Drake takes such pride in everything running so smoothly at his resort."

"Yes, well, Drake's not so happy with me right now. He probably told Bernard to take his sweet time coming back for us."

"Why isn't Drake happy with you?"

"He asked to sleep with my wife tonight. When I told him no, he became annoyed."

B.J.'s eyes rounded comically. "He did *what?*"

"Of course, if you're interested, I could always tell him I changed my mind."

The paperback hit him squarely in the chest. "You jerk. You made that up just to rattle me."

He grinned, pleased to see the reluctant amusement in her eyes. "I told you you'd call me that again."

GINA WILKINS

"Now I'm convinced again that it was you who put the snake in my bag."

Still smiling, he set the book aside. "Nope. I laughed my butt off, but I didn't do it."

"Mmm." She looked at him as though she were still reserving judgment on his guilt.

He wanted to kiss her. The urge was suddenly so strong he could almost taste her already.

Perhaps something of his thoughts appeared in his expression. B.J.'s smile slowly faded as she studied his face.

"Stop it," she said almost fiercely.

"I'm not doing anything."

"You're giving me that look. The one you use when you're putting on an act for Drake and his men."

His annoyance that she thought he was acting at the moment goaded him into speaking more candidly than he should have. "I'm not pretending to be attracted to you, if that's what you mean."

Her cheeks warmed, but her scowl only deepened. "If this is your way of distracting me from questioning you about your dealings with Drake, don't bother. I've decided I don't even want to know now."

She was irritating him more with every accusation. "Do you really find it so hard to believe that I find you attractive?"

"Let's just say I doubt I'm your usual type."

He had to admit, if only to himself, that she was right about that. His "usual type" would be someone who was worldly, sophisticated and who would expect nothing more from him than a few hours of companion-ship. Someone more like Ingrid, to be honest, though he'd had trouble noticing Ingrid's charms when B.J. had been nearby.

But actually his general boredom with his "usual type" had resulted in increasingly lengthy stretches of celibacy during the past couple of years. It had just seemed easier to focus on business rather than to pur-sue one meaningless encounter after another.

As for anything more meaningful—well, he hadn't been willing to risk that. From his experience, loving someone was just too painful. He doubted that B.J. would understand, despite the uncanny insight she sometimes displayed about him.

Because he had no intention of being the one who broke her vulnerable, trusting heart, he abruptly stood and began to pace restlessly around the shelter, watch-ing the water for any sign of Bernard. It wasn't dark yet, but the shadows were definitely growing longer and deeper. Would Drake actually go as far as leaving them here overnight to make his point?

Oh, yeah. And they should probably consider them-selves fortunate if that was the extent of the lesson.

Still sitting in the lounge chair, B.J. watched Daniel openly as he prowled through the shelter like a caged cat. Several times he checked his watch and once he pulled his cell phone out of his pants pocket. His low growl of frustration told her that he wasn't getting a signal.

When he seemed to become too confined by the stone floor, he stepped down onto the sand and began to pace the beach, sidestepping the rock-lined fire pit off to one side of the pavilion.

The more time she spent with him, the more he confused her. At one moment he seemed so familiar to her, so much like the Daniel she had known before. And then, almost at the blink of an eye, he changed, becoming an enigmatic stranger.

A stranger who claimed to be attracted to her.

She tried to observe him objectively. He stood framed against the deepening blue sky, his thick, black hair rumpled around his face. His white shirt, which contrasted so appealingly with his brown skin, was plastered to his chest by the stiff breeze from the ocean.

Studying the ridges of bone and muscle outlined by the thin fabric, she felt her pulse rate increase. So much for objectivity.

She had never denied to herself that she was attracted to him. From the moment she'd seen him standing on the staircase at the farmhouse—hell, from the time she'd been fourteen years old—his effect on her had been powerful.

She found it hard to believe he could feel the same way about her. And yet she hadn't forgotten the heat generated by the kisses that had passed between them. It hadn't all been an act, on either of their parts.

As improbable as it seemed, there was a bond between them. One that had been formed a long time ago. The question now was, what were they going to do about it?

She doubted that he was interested in—or was used to—anything more than a brief fling. Scratching an itch. Satisfying his curiosity. Some other cliché that translated to no-strings sex.

And really what more could she expect? She certainly had no intention of playing Ingrid to his Drake. Waiting patiently for his attention, content to enjoy his money without questioning where it came from. No way.

The sky was growing darker, and it was now quite dim within the shadow of the pavilion. Bernard was definitely taking his time coming back for them. She was going to have to hurry now to shower and change before Ingrid's show.

Another fifteen minutes of silence passed before Daniel turned on the beach and headed back toward her. Something in his expression brought her to her feet. "What?"

"I think you should be prepared for the possibility that we'll be spending the night here."

His voice was steady and uninflected, but she didn't for a moment suspect that he was teasing. He was completely serious.

"Should I be worried?" she asked, trying to speak as matter-of-factly as he had.

"No. We'll be safe here. And I'm sure Bernard will show up early tomorrow with an elaborate story about how we were 'accidentally' stranded here."

"Do you have any idea why we're being, um, accidentally stranded here?"

He nodded grimly. "It's a message, of course. I haven't been cooperating with Drake today, and he's giving me a little illustration of how easily he could make us disappear."

"You aren't cooperating?"

She had tried to disguise her sudden surge of hope, but Daniel must have caught it. He shook his head. "I'm not pulling out of the deal. I'm just jerking him around to get a better cut for myself—and he knows it."

Disappointed, she asked, "So this is his way of retaliating?"

He glanced at his watch and then at the setting sun. "I believe it is. I had a bad feeling about this picnic from the beginning."

"*Now* you tell me."

"I'm sorry, B.J. I didn't really think he'd pull a stunt like this with you involved. But I'm sure he figures that bringing you into it makes his warning even more ominous for me."

"Men and their posturing," she grumbled with a scowl.

"The hell of it is, he was absolutely right. Doing this to you is much more effective than anything he could have used to threaten me."

"You said we aren't in any danger."

"No. We'll be fine here. Not particularly comfortable, but safe."

"We'll miss Ingrid's performance."

"That's probably just a side benefit to Drake. He was ticked with you and her both for backing him into that corner."

"Have I mentioned that I can't stand that guy?"

"I wouldn't call him my favorite pal either."

"Then why don't you cut your losses and get away from the creep? We can leave as soon as we get back tomorrow—whenever that might be."

Daniel sighed gustily and pushed a hand through his hair. "It's too late for that."

"No, it's not." She took a step closer to him, speaking with an urgency that seemed to grip her by the heart. "You can come back to Texas with me. My uncles can help you with Drake if he becomes a problem. Talk to Jared. I'm sure he'll be able to…well—"

"Reform me?" Daniel supplied ironically. And then he shook his head. "The thing is, I don't want to be reformed, B.J."

"But—"

"Look." His voice was rough now. "Don't mistake me for the confused kid I used to be. I'm not looking for a foster home now or a mentor. I'm making my own life—and I don't need anyone giving me guidance in how to do it."

Including her. The unspoken addition seemed to hang in the air between them.

Wrapping her arms around herself, she turned away from him. "Fine. If you would rather model yourself after Judson Drake than Jared Walker, you have every right to do so."

"*Damn it,* B.J." He seemed to want to say more, but he bit off whatever it might have been and turned abruptly toward the storage cabinets at the back of the shelter. "I saw some lighters in one of the cabinets. I'll see if I can get the torches burning before it gets dark."

He had sounded oddly insulted by her comment, she thought speculatively, watching him stalk across the rough stone floor. But he shouldn't hold his breath waiting for her to apologize.

She thought the world of her uncle, a former Navy man turned rancher whose tough, work-weathered exterior hid a heart as big as the Texas sky. Though he had always provided for his family—and made time for the troubled boys who had drifted through his life—Jared would never have access to the kind of money or social status that Drake commanded. But when it came to character, Drake wasn't worthy of wiping the dust from her uncle's boots.

It broke her heart to think that Daniel had been more impressed by Drake's flashy posturing than Jared's quiet, steady decency.

Daniel hadn't become the man she had hoped to find. And she realized sadly that she'd brought entirely too many adolescent fantasies along with her on this search.

The torchlights flickered brightly, casting a golden glow through the pavilion and into the immediate surrounding area. Daniel had lit them all, as well as the logs that had been stacked in the fire pit, providing enough light that B.J. probably could have read again, had she been able to concentrate on the story.

Standing outside the pavilion, she could see stars

gleaming in the black-velvet sky and the white crests of waves lapping against the sand. It was a blatantly romantic setting. There was certainly nothing outwardly threatening about the situation. Which made the underlying message all the more insidious.

"We have plenty more food, if you want a snack," Daniel said, stepping out of the shelter to join her. "Cookies and pastries or fruit and cheese and crackers. There are more cold sodas and bottled waters, too."

She started to refuse and then she changed her mind. It wasn't as if there was much else to do. She might as well have a cookie.

"You know, I really love chocolate for a late-evening snack," she said with a regretful sigh after swallowing a bit of crispy almond cookie. "That was truly malicious of you to tell Creepy Guy I'm allergic to chocolate."

"You started it with that big tale about me being lactose intolerant," he retorted. "Just like your grandfather," he added in a mutter.

She couldn't help laughing at the memory of his expression when she'd said that—not to mention the looks Drake and Ingrid had given her. "Sorry, but I thought I deserve to get in one low blow, considering everything."

"You deserve a lot more than that. Especially now that I've gotten you stranded here for a night. I wouldn't blame you if you found a coconut and knocked me upside the head with it."

His rueful tone made her smile again. She was glad they weren't still verbally sniping at each other. Since they were here for the duration of the night, the time

would pass much more pleasantly if they got along—
which meant she should butt out of his business, she advised herself. After all, she was the one who had
stumbled into his life and put both him and his mysterious plans at risk.

Once this night was over and she had returned to her
life in Dallas, she would put the old daydreams behind
her and write Daniel off as a lost cause, she promised
herself. She doubted she would ever see him again. He
could try to buy himself happiness, and she would try
to find her own through other means—her work, for example. Her family.

And maybe instead of being disappointed with what
Daniel had become, she would take some pleasure in
remembering a few exciting, if risky, days with the
dashing boy of her girlhood dreams.

Chapter Nine

By nine-thirty it seemed quite clear that Bernard wouldn't be returning for them that night. "I guess you were right," B.J. said after checking her watch. "We're here for the night. And we've missed Ingrid's show. I hope it went well for her."

Daniel looked up from the playing cards in his hand. They had unearthed a wooden box from one cabinet earlier, discovering that it held playing cards, poker chips, a set of dominoes, checkers and chess pieces and a backgammon board. Daniel figured the games were to entertain guests during the frequent but usually quite brief autumn showers that kept the vegetation so lush and green.

B.J. had pounced rather eagerly on the games, probably relieved that they had something to occupy them to make the time they spent together less awkward.

"You're still worrying about missing Ingrid's performance?"

"Well...I did promise. And I hate to think there were no friendly faces in the audience for her."

Daniel laid his cards in front of him and rested his elbows on the table, studying her over his loosely clasped hands. "I'm glad to know the nice girl I remembered has turned into an equally nice woman."

He'd meant it as a simple compliment. He didn't expect B.J. to set her cards down with a scowl and push herself abruptly to her feet. "I'm thirsty again. Do you want anything?"

"No, I'm okay." He watched moodily as she opened the cooler and drew out a half bottle of water she had opened earlier.

Why had it bothered her so badly that he'd commented about how well she'd turned out? Was it because she wasn't able to say the same thing about him?

If you would rather model yourself after Judson Drake than Jared Walker, you have every right to do so.

Beneath the table his hands drew into fists on his knees. She didn't understand, of course. She couldn't possibly understand, having come from such a drastically different background.

He continued to watch her as she walked to the fire pit. She had donned her cardigan as a shield against the cooler night air. She sat on the sand with her arms wrapped around her upraised knees, the water bottle un-

touched on the sand beside her. Her somber expression
was illuminated by the leaping flames.

Damn, but she was beautiful. Funny how he hadn't
seen that at the beginning, thinking then that she was
merely pretty. Cute. The more time he spent with her,
the more he appreciated the genuine beauty of her—
both inward and outward.

Yet she was openly disappointed with the man he had
become. She saw him as more closely resembling Judson Drake than Jared Walker, the uncle she revered.

The hell of it was, he couldn't entirely disagree
with her.

Sitting by a campfire had always made her rather mel-
ancholy. Now she found herself swamped with nostalgia,
thinking of the campfires at the Walker ranch. Muted
laughter and the steady rumble of adult conversation.
Children's eager chattering. Camp songs. Roasted marsh-
mallows drawn blackened and melting from the flames.

Her brother and sister and parents, aunts, uncles and
cousins. Family. As often as she had felt suffocated by
the sheer number of them, she found herself missing
them all now.

Was her mother worrying about her? Layla Walker
Samples was a notorious worrier, especially when it
came to her three kids—all of whom had occasionally
given her cause for concern. Layla would be wondering what was going on now, since it was so uncharac-
teristic for B.J. to just take off on her own.

B.J. wouldn't be at all surprised if her uncles were

looking for her despite the explanatory e-mail she had sent home.

She wished she could talk to her mother now. Or even better, her father. The dependable, pragmatic accountant was the one person B.J. could always count on for calm, rational, objective advice.

"Are you cold?" Daniel asked as he knelt beside her.

Her chin resting on her up-drawn knees, B.J. did not look away from the flames. "No."

"You aren't nervous about being here tonight?"

"No, of course not. I've camped out plenty of times before."

Sensing that he was still looking at her in concern, she lifted her head to look at him. "I'm fine, Daniel. I guess I was just a little homesick for a minute there."

He glanced from her face to the fire. "Remembering the campfires at the ranch?"

It was odd to hear him put her thoughts into words, as if he'd had a glimpse into her memories. "Yes."

"I remember them, too. I enjoyed them, as much as I enjoyed anything during that time."

"You always sat on the outer edges, as far away from everyone else as Jared would allow. You never joined in the songs or the storytelling."

"I didn't know how. Cozy family gatherings were a new experience for me."

"You were so angry. It seemed like you were always scowling."

"I *was* angry," he agreed. "But you never seemed to worry that I would take it out on you."

"No."

"Why not?"

She hesitated a moment, then answered candidly, "Because of the way you treated Molly. She was only eleven and going through that pesky, chattery stage, but even though I could tell she got on your nerves sometimes, you never snapped at her."

He looked surprised. "She was just a kid. A little spoiled, maybe, but she always meant well. I remember going to fairly elaborate lengths to avoid her when I wasn't in the mood for her babbling—which was fairly often—but I could never really be angry with her."

"No one ever could. That hasn't changed, by the way."

"I could never figure out why Jared and Cassie took in problem foster boys when they had a little girl in their house. They were taking a pretty big chance with that, weren't they?"

B.J. shrugged. "More than a few people expressed concern about that during the years Molly was growing up. But really she had Jared and Shane watching every move she made, and Cassie always nearby. No boy had the nerve to even try anything under those circumstances. Even when she passed sixteen and turned into a real beauty, she never had a problem with the foster boys. She complained that she was probably the most closely guarded teenager in Texas."

Daniel chuckled. "I suppose she was. I always knew Shane would take my head off if I even looked cross-eyed at his baby sister—and that was assuming Jared didn't pound me into dust first. Hell, by the time I left, *I* was watching out for her like a big brother."

"She was very fond of you, you know. They all were. Molly cried after you left."

"From what I understand, she cried every time one of the foster boys left."

"Well…yeah," B.J. admitted. "But she did miss you. We…they all did."

If he noticed the slight stammer, he ignored it. Instead he tossed another stick into the fire pit. The wood began to burn with a pop and a crackle. Only thing missing was a snap, B.J. mused, propping her chin on her knees again.

"So…you want to play another game? Checkers? Chess?"

"No, thanks." She continued to gaze solemnly into the fire. "I think I'll just sit here for a while."

She felt his gaze on her, but she didn't look away from the flames. After a moment Daniel stood, brushing sand off his pants. "I'll start squaring away the pavilion. Find us a place to sleep. No, don't get up. I can handle it."

She relaxed again, deciding not to argue with him. She let her mind drift again, and though she made a conscious effort to avoid dwelling on old memories and fantasies, those thoughts weren't so easy to dispel.

Daniel rigged makeshift beds by laying out chair cushions on the picnic tables. A flashlight unearthed from one of the cupboards gave B.J. enough light to make use of the now-dark ladies' room.

After helping B.J. onto one of the tables, Daniel extinguished most of the torches, threw another couple of logs in the fire pit, then climbed onto the other table. "Not particularly comfortable, is it?"

B.J. lay on her side, cradling her head on one arm. "It's not too bad."

On the other table, Daniel lay facing her, mimicking her position. Shadows cloaked him so that she couldn't really see his face, nor did she imagine he could see hers any better. "Are you too chilly?"

"A light blanket would feel pretty good, but my cardigan should be warm enough."

"Sorry there's no blanket. You'd think with all the other stuff Drake stocks in those cupboards, he'd at least have one or two."

"I'll be okay."

"Let me know if you need anything during the night."

"Thanks." She closed her eyes, trying to will herself to sleep. It wasn't going to be easy, what with the hard table, the cool air, the sounds of the ocean and the night-calling birds. Not to mention Daniel lying so close to her.

Apparently she managed to doze. She woke with a start when she realized that she was no longer alone on the narrow table. "What—"

"You were shivering," Daniel murmured, wrapping an arm around her. "I don't have a blanket, but I can offer body heat."

She *was* cold, she realized groggily. She had drawn into a tight ball on the cushions and she was shivering. Daniel's warmth against her back felt good, but still—

"I don't think this is a very good idea."

"We're just going to sleep," he assured her, nestling her more snugly against him. "We've slept together before. Our first night here, remember?"

Yes, but that had been in a bed. A bed so large they'd slept the entire night without even brushing against each other.

"Go to sleep, B.J. Tomorrow is soon enough to start fretting again."

It seemed easier to do as he suggested than to argue. Enjoying the warmth wrapped around her, she let herself sink into oblivion again.

It wasn't quite dawn the next time she awoke. The sky was just beginning to lighten to charcoal rather than the inky black of midnight. And she and Daniel were nestled more snugly than two pages in a closed book.

Holding her breath, she lay very still, trying to decide if he was asleep. His breathing was deep and even, each slow exhale brushing against the back of her neck like a teasing caress.

Through her clothing she felt the warmth radiating from his body. A body she could feel in some detail. Biceps, pecs, abs—the man was definitely well-developed from waist up.

As for waist down—

His thighs were solid against the backs of hers. And the bulge against her hip was substantial.

"Are you awake?" His voice was a low rumble in her ear.

Oh, yeah. She was suddenly wide awake. "Uh-huh," was all she managed to say.

"Cold?"

Hardly. "Uh-uh."

"Did you get any sleep?"

"Some. You?"

"Couple hours. I guess a hard picnic table can be pretty comfortable, huh?"

She moistened her lips. "Apparently."

Without thinking, she shifted her weight. The movement pressed her more snugly against his groin, a wholly unpremeditated result.

"Then again," Daniel said, his voice suddenly hoarse, "maybe it's not so comfortable, after all."

She moved instinctively to shift into a less intimate position. Unfortunately Daniel moved at the same time, and they ended up more entangled than before.

B.J. froze before she could get into even more trouble. There was just enough light for her to see Daniel's rather pained expression. She knew she must look mortified.

"Maybe we should just get up," she said in exasperation.

His sudden crooked smile flashed, and even in the faint light she could see the wickedness in it. He didn't have to say a word.

She forced herself to frown at him, trying to speak evenly despite the rapid beating of her heart. "Behave yourself."

"I know I should," he murmured reflectively. But he didn't move.

B.J. felt her throat tighten. "Um...Daniel?"

"Yeah. I'm going to move now." But instead he brushed a strand of hair away from her face and remained where he was, looming over her, bodies touching from chest to ankles. Touching intimately enough that she could tell he was becoming more aroused by the moment.

She put a hand on his chest. Probably to push him away. At least, so she tried to tell herself. Instead her fingers curled into his shirt, slowly kneading the warm skin beneath the thin fabric.

Oh, he was strong. Solid. A man one could lean on. Curl into.

But not one she could completely trust, she reminded herself in an attempt to quell the desire rising inside her.

It didn't work. When Daniel lowered his head, she lifted hers to meet him.

Their previous kisses had begun with an audience in mind. Though the embraces had threatened to spin out of control nearly every time, there had always been the awareness of onlookers, the reality of the roles they were playing to keep them reined in.

There was no audience this time, no reason to perform. And nothing to stop them except willpower—which, B.J. conceded, wasn't going to be enough.

She had been fantasizing about this man, this moment, for almost half her life.

Resting his weight on one elbow, he cupped her face between his hands, tilting her head to provide him unrestricted access to her mouth. He spent a long time exploring her lips, nibbling at them, tasting them, tracing them with the tip of his tongue. And then parting them so that he could delve more deeply.

His tongue swept the inside of her mouth, tangled with hers, then taunted with slow, rhythmic thrusts that made her hips move instinctively in tempo. Murmuring something that might have been an attempt to soothe her, he slid a hand down her stomach. His fingers spread across her abdomen, resting so close to that aching place between her legs that she moaned helplessly into his mouth.

Entreaty turning to demand, she speared her hands into his luxuriously thick hair and kissed him with a renewed fervor. She sensed his control slipping away from him. Heard it in the ragged edges of his increasingly rapid breathing. Felt it in the hammering of his heart against her ribs. Her own was beating so hard and so fast that she knew he could feel it, too.

His fingers moved an inch lower, and she arched in response, one knee rising to cradle him more intimately between her thighs. There was no pretending now that either of them was in control. No way for either of them to deny the need that was driving them.

"B.J.," he muttered against her throat.

She was so very glad he hadn't called her Brittany. That he wanted the woman she had become. Sliding her hands beneath his shirt, she stroked the warm, supple skin of his back and kissed him again. Only this time it was slow, not fevered. Deliberate, not impetuous.

She didn't think she could make the invitation more clear.

He froze for just a moment against her. Just long enough for her to sense the battle taking place inside him. Hunger warred with common sense—and she was so deeply relieved when need won out. When his head lowered again to her throat, there was no mistaking the new purpose in his actions.

He kissed a path from her jaw to her ear, took a tiny, arousing nip of her earlobe, then dipped his tongue into the hollow behind it. More kisses led downward to the deep V of her blouse, toward the rise of her breasts, which were already heaving with the breaths she struggled to drag into her lungs. Her attention was divided between the journey he was taking with his mouth and the movement of his fingers against her tummy, her thighs and—finally—against the so-sensitive area between them.

She jerked spasmodically in reaction, gasping his name. Once again his mouth returned to hers, attempting to calm her but succeeding only in making her want more.

"Don't stop," she said when he lifted his head, breaking the kiss.

His gaze bore into hers, his dark eyes glittering in the pale gray light of predawn. "Be sure," he said roughly. "I won't apologize later."

"I won't ask you to," she said and moved deliberately against the hard bulge at her hip. The involuntary grunt of reaction she drew from him filled her with a satisfying sense of feminine power, giving her the courage to move again.

Whatever thin hold he'd had over his control seemed

to snap then. The man she had thought incapable of acting without careful deliberation proved that he could be as blindly driven by passion as any other mere mortal.

His hands were all over her, drawing away her clothes and the unsteadiness in them thrilled her. His movements were jerky, primal, unpremeditated—yet so innately skillful they took her straight to the edge of sanity.

They plunged over that edge together, filling the shadows in the quiet pavilion with cries of exhilaration. And maybe just a touch of anxiety—on both their parts—at what might come after the landing.

The sky had lightened to a pearly gray-blue by the time B.J. recovered enough to think coherently. Blinking dazedly, she took mental stock of her situation.

Both only half-clothed, she and Daniel lay still sprawled together on the cushion-padded picnic table. Her head rested on his shoulder and her fingers were curled into a death grip on his partially opened shirt. His heart was still beating loudly beneath her ear, but the rate was gradually slowing to normal. His breathing was almost steady now, as was her own.

Yet she knew that some things would never return to the way they had been before. Her heart, for example.

"We didn't use protection," Daniel said, and there was just a hint of disbelief in his voice, as though he was stunned that the realization had only just occurred to him.

Hoping that meant he wasn't usually so careless, B.J. reassured him, "It's okay. I'm on the Pill."

She saw no need to add that she took the Pill more for cramp relief than an active social life.

She felt his shoulders relax just a fraction and sensed his relief that the repercussions of their lovemaking would only be emotional ones. "I'm not apologizing..."

"Good. I don't want you to," she said rather fiercely.

"...but," he continued, ignoring her interjection, "I hope you won't have any regrets later."

"I knew what I was doing. I won't regret it," she managed to say evenly, hoping she was telling the truth. Knowing it was true now, at least.

He muttered something that sounded like, "I hope *I* won't," but before she could ask him to repeat it—or explain—he was moving. Shifting his weight from beneath her, he rolled to his feet, reaching for scattered articles of clothing.

"I'll be right back," he said without looking at her and disappeared into the men's room.

A bit disoriented by how abruptly he had abandoned her, B.J. sat up and ran a shaking hand through her wildly tumbled hair. She hadn't expected a declaration of undying devotion, or even flowery, romantic sweet nothings, but a "Wow, that was great," would have been nice. A couple more kisses, maybe.

Closing herself into the ladies' room with her wrinkled clothes and her tattered pride, she reminded herself that she had promised there would be no regrets. She hadn't been lying—she couldn't regret something that had been so exciting and spectacular, so close to the fantasies she had never expected to experience.

Which wasn't to say there wouldn't be moments of wistfulness that the inevitable conclusion couldn't have been different for them.

A boat arrived for them just after daybreak. It wasn't Bernard at the helm this time, but a young man who seemed braced for unpleasantness when they approached him.

"My name is Greg. Mr. Drake asked me to convey his most sincere apologies for your inconvenience," he recited quickly, before Daniel or B.J. had a chance to speak. "There was a mix-up in communications, and it was believed that a boat had been sent for you last night. It was only this morning that anyone realized you were still on the island. We sincerely hope there was no harm done during the hours you spent here."

Glaring at the young man, Daniel considered knocking him on his butt—just for the satisfaction of punching someone. It would make a nice demonstration for B.J. that he didn't take Drake's threatening gestures lightly, especially when they involved her. But taking his anger out on someone who'd had nothing to do with stranding them here would accomplish nothing.

He would vent his temper toward those who deserved it, he decided, turning away. But not before he saw the quick relief cross Greg's face; he must have read the violent impulse in Daniel's eyes.

Making sure B.J. was settled comfortably on the launch, he took a seat across from her rather than beside her. He didn't quite trust himself to sit close to her yet.

This trip would pass all too quickly, and then it would be time again for them to resume their roles as devoted spouses. It would take him that long to get his impassive mask firmly back into place, his long-buried emotions safely hidden away again.

No harm done? Greg had no idea just how much damage those hours on the island had caused. Emotional barriers that had taken years to build and fortify were now deeply cracked, and there was no telling how long it would take him to repair them.

Daniel was afraid they would never be quite as safe and impenetrable as they had been before.

Chapter Ten

The Daniel Andreas who stepped off the boat at the resort marina was not the same man who had made passionate love to B.J. such a short time before. This man was hard, tensed, jaw set and eyes snapping with temper.

Dangerous.

He had said very little to her since they'd emerged from the pavilion restrooms. He had given her a few terse instructions about how to behave when they returned to the resort—basically, she was to appear bewildered and confused. But there had been no personal conversation at all. No discussion about what had passed between them.

From the way Daniel was acting now, they might as well have spent the entire night on separate islands.

Bernard stepped forward to greet them at the marina. He wore his usual summer-weight boxy jacket with a T-shirt and pressed jeans, and even though it was very early, his bald head was already shiny with perspiration.

He greeted them with an expression of patently false sincerity. "I'm so sorry you were accidentally stranded. There was a mix-up about who was supposed to—"

Daniel's fist connected with Bernard's jaw, rocking the bigger man's head back and cutting off the sentence midword. Even as B.J. gasped in shock at the speed of the strike, another jacketed man appeared seemingly out of nowhere, moving toward Daniel with deadly purpose.

She threw herself at Daniel, catching his arm and tugging him away from Bernard. "Daniel Andreas! Have you lost your mind?"

"That," Daniel said without looking away from Bernard, "was for the discomfort my wife suffered during the night."

"For heaven's sake, Daniel, that wasn't necessary." B.J. was playing her role with a note of desperation now. "You heard Bernard say it was all a misunderstanding."

The deep flush of temper slowly receded from Bernard's face as he glanced at B.J. Jerking his chin to send the newcomer on his way, he wiped at his lower lip with the back of one hand, smearing a tiny trickle of blood.

Playing rapidly on her advantage, she spoke again.

"I must apologize for my husband, Bernard. He tends to be overprotective when it comes to me."

"There's no need for you to apologize, Mrs. Andreas. A man must protect his most valuable asset, isn't that right, Daniel?"

Daniel's arm twitched again, as if he was strongly tempted to hit Bernard again. B.J. held on tightly, her heart in her throat.

"I want to talk to Drake," Daniel growled. "Now."

"I'm sorry, Mr. Drake is away from the resort this morning. I'm sure he'll want to meet with you as soon as he returns."

"That's just as well," B.J. said firmly. "It will give my husband a chance to get his temper under control."

She tried to inject wifely exasperation into her tone, calling on memories of her mother's voice when she was annoyed with her husband of more than thirty years.

Bernard motioned toward the walkway that led back to their suite. "I'm sure you'd like to rest and freshen up. Coffee and brunch will be sent to your suite as soon as you let the staff know you're ready."

"Thank you," B.J. said, keeping a firm grip on Daniel's arm. "We would like to go to our suite for a while. Come along, Daniel."

She was almost surprised when he complied without further resistance.

B.J. was prepared by now for Daniel to sweep the rooms for listening devices when they returned, and he did so swiftly. Only then did he return to where she waited in the sitting room.

"You played that scene with Bernard perfectly," he surprised her by saying. "Exactly the way I hoped you would."

"Who was playing?" she demanded, planting her fists on her hips to stare at him. "I thought he was going to pound you into the sand. And then order that other guy to shoot you to finish you off. Did you *see* the look on Bernard's face when you hit him? He was furious."

With a rueful look on his face, Daniel flexed his right hand. "The guy's got a jaw made of granite. I thought I'd crushed my knuckles."

"Then why did you hit him?"

He shrugged. "I can't afford to be seen as weak in front of these guys. They know *I* know we were stranded there deliberately. I couldn't let it pass without striking back."

"This whole situation just gets more ridiculous by the minute," she muttered, turning away in disgust. "I swear men have a broken chromosome or something that makes them act like idiots."

"You won't hear any argument from me," he replied with an undertone of amusement. "But since that's the equipment that was issued to me, I've got to make the most of it if I want to win the game."

"Let me guess. The one who dies with the most toys wins?"

"Close. The one who stays alive longest with the most toys wins."

"And the one who gets killed trying to collect those toys?" she asked in little more than a whisper.

"That guy should have stayed on the bench."

Moistening her lips, she looked over her shoulder at him. "And what about the people who get in the way?"

After only a slight hesitation he answered, "Usually, even despite the player's best intentions, they get run over."

Having carried the strained metaphor as far as she could take it, B.J. turned abruptly toward the bedroom. "I'm going to take a shower."

He made no move to detain her.

Ten minutes later she stood with her eyes closed and her face turned into the warm water cascading from the brass-plated shower head. The shower soothed her skin and relaxed her tight muscles, but it couldn't wash away the memories of the previous night that would probably haunt her for the rest of her life. Nor could it dilute the fear that something terrible would happen to Daniel if he continued on his present course—whatever that was.

When Daniel's big hands closed gently on her shoulders, she gasped, nearly inhaling a mouthful of water. She had forgotten how very silently he could move. How unpredictably he could behave. And when those hands slid around to gently cup her small, wet breasts, she moaned and went liquid in his arms.

"It occurred to me," he murmured against the back of her neck, "that I never told you how special this morning was for me."

She leaned back against him. "No, you didn't."

"It was—" he turned her in his arms and gazed down into her eyes with a tender smile "—spectacular."

She couldn't stay annoyed with him when he spoke in that particular tone. When he looked at her in that particular way. She wrapped her arms around his neck and lifted her mouth to his.

Hands slid avidly over wet, slick skin, pausing often to explore and caress. B.J. wrapped her leg around his, locking them together, savoring the roughness of his hair against her smooth skin, the bulge of muscle in his calf. The position pressed them together from chest to knees, and she reveled in the differences between them. The way they fit so perfectly together.

She had been self-conscious at first, worried that Daniel would be disappointed with her lack of voluptuous curves. Yet the appreciation on his face when he looked at her, when he touched her, when he slid down to explore her sleek body with his mouth, reassured her that her slender form appealed to him.

The water was beginning to cool, but B.J.'s temperature was rising. She wouldn't have been at all surprised to see steam rising from her skin.

She speared her hands into his wet hair, her back arching when he pressed openmouthed kisses on her thighs. "Daniel?"

He rose to his feet and reached behind her to turn off the water. "Last time we hurried a bit," he murmured. "Now we're going to take our time."

She didn't know why he had changed again from cool and distant to warm and passionate. She could hardly keep up with his mood swings, never really knew when he was playing a role and when he was being himself. If ever. If she had any sense, she would be pushing him away, protecting herself from falling even harder for him than she already had.

Apparently she had no sense at all when it came to Daniel.

Barely taking time to towel off, they fell onto the bed they had shared so platonically before. Despite what Daniel had said in the shower, B.J. expected things to progress rapidly from that point.

Instead he slowed down, taking a leisurely journey of nibbling kisses from her throat to her toes and then back again. He cupped her face between his hands and kissed her mouth, her eyelids, the tip of her nose. But still he didn't hurry.

When she could stand it no longer, when she began to wonder if he was ever going to satisfy the ravenous hunger inside her, she rolled fiercely onto him and took matters into her own hands. So to speak.

Soon it was Daniel who was groaning. Demanding. And B.J. was the one who taunted and teased, giving only so much before drawing back and leaving him aching for more.

His skin glistened with sweat when he finally snapped, when the control that was so much a part of him deserted him. She marveled at the wildness in his eyes when he flipped her beneath him, and then the wildness took charge of her own mind, depriving her of coherent thought.

* * *

B.J. had barely recovered her breath when someone knocked on the door to the sitting room. She opened her eyes just as Daniel pushed himself upright.

"That will be our brunch," he said, straightening his disordered hair with a sweep of his hand. "I'll get it."

Their lovemaking had left her drowsy and lethargic, but the mention of food reenergized her. She sat up, the sheet falling to her waist. "Great, I'm hungry."

Daniel chuckled roughly and leaned over to kiss her, one hand brushing her bare breast in the process. His expression when he drew away made it clear that the intimate contact had not been accidental. "Why does that not surprise me?"

He wrapped himself in a thick terry bathrobe and headed for the other room. Pulling her own robe around her, B.J. took only a minute to ruffle her tumbled, mostly dry hair into place before following him, hoping there would be Belgian waffles on the brunch tray.

But it wasn't room service standing just inside the door in the sitting room. It was Judson Drake.

B.J. froze. Drake's cool eyes swept her from head to toe, and she knew she must look as though she had just crawled out of bed. Since Daniel looked the same way, it must have been obvious what they'd been doing before Drake arrived. She felt her cheeks flame.

The scene worked perfectly into the false stories Daniel had woven about them, of course. Yet surely he couldn't have predicted Drake would find them this way. She didn't want to believe there was anything pre-meditated in the way Daniel had made love to her.

"Mrs. Andreas." Drake's voice held a faint note of mockery that set her teeth on edge. "I just stopped by to express my deepest apologies at the incompetence of my staff in leaving you stranded on the island all night. I understand your husband was justifiably infuriated on your behalf earlier. Fortunately his temper seems to have been…soothed since his encounter with Bernard."

Because she didn't quite trust herself to respond without ruining everything, B.J. merely crossed her arms over her chest and nodded.

"My wife is hungry and she needs time to recuper-ate from our ordeal," Daniel said bluntly. "If you'll ex-cuse us…"

"Of course. As a matter of fact, here's your food now." Drake moved out of the way to allow a uniformed server to push in a fully loaded tray. "Please let me know if there is anything at all I can do to make it up to you, Mrs. Andreas. And, Daniel, I trust you'll be able to meet with me this afternoon while your wife rests?"

"It would serve you right if I caught the first shuttle out of this place," Daniel growled, making B.J.'s heart jump with a foolish optimism.

Drake's left eyebrow rose. "That would be unfortu-nate," he murmured, "for both of us."

Daniel allowed another couple of moments to pass in silence and then he nodded shortly. "I'll see you later. But right now I'd like to attend to my wife."

"Most certainly." Drake took a step toward B.J., obviously intending to take her hand or rest a hand on her shoulder or some other meaningless gesture of sincerity. She and Daniel moved at the same moment—she took a step back from Drake just as Daniel stepped between them.

"I'll see you later," Daniel repeated to Drake.

The other man paused, his eyes narrowing in temper, but then he nodded. "Mrs. Andreas," he said and gave her a stiff little bow before taking his leave. The bellman left immediately afterward.

"I'm not sure I'm hungry now," B.J. said with a shudder.

Daniel was already uncovering fragrant dishes. "Belgian waffles," he said enticingly. "With fresh berries and bacon. Or you might prefer an omelet. Or maybe…"

She sighed gustily. "Okay, maybe I can eat," she muttered, her stomach giving a soft rumble of concurrence. "But that guy still creeps me out."

Saying nothing, Daniel poured steaming coffee into two china cups and waved her into her seat at the table.

They ate for a few minutes in silence. The food was delicious, but B.J. had to make an effort to appreciate it. "Why do you always treat me like a not-very-bright child in front of Creepy Guy?"

Daniel shrugged. "Sorry. It fits our cover story."

"What woman would really appreciate being treated that way?"

"You'd be surprised," he answered drily. "Some

women want nothing more than to be petted and pampered."

"I can't see you being interested in a woman like that."

"No. I wouldn't be."

"Just as I wouldn't be interested in one of those men who needs constant ego stroking and kowtowing by the women in his life. I bet Drake's like that."

"Definitely." Daniel took a sip of his coffee, then asked casually, "So what type of man are you looking for?"

"I'm not looking," she answered tartly. "But if I do meet someone who interests me, it will be a man who treats me as an equal. Who values my intelligence and my opinions. Who wouldn't want to change me into some Hollywood ideal of the perfect woman."

"Any man who doesn't value you exactly the way you are isn't worth your attention."

She looked up from her food in response to the quiet comment. But before she could say anything, Daniel was talking again, abruptly changing the subject. "I'll be meeting with Drake for several hours this afternoon. It might be best if you stay in the suite to, um, recover from your ordeal."

"Oh, give me a break. Even the wimpy woman you made up for Drake's benefit would hardly have to take to her bed for an entire day just because she'd had to spend a night outdoors."

"Still, I'd feel better if you stay away from Bernard and Drake's other employees today. At least when I'm not around."

Her head rose sharply. Even though he'd spoken lightly, there was something in his voice that made her pulse jump. "Is there some reason I should be concerned?"

"I just don't like the possibility that you could be used as leverage against me," he admitted. "Leaving us on that island was a warning. The next one won't be so subtle."

"Will there be a next one?"

"Not if I play my part shrewdly. But I'd like you to keep the doors locked, anyway. Put out the Do Not Disturb sign and take a few hours to rest, watch television, read. Even though I realize you aren't so delicate to be harmed by a night of camping out, you're probably tired anyway. It wouldn't hurt you to spend a lazy afternoon."

She didn't like the thought of being ordered to stay in her room, but she wasn't thrilled about the possibility of crossing Bernard's path either. It wasn't as if there was anything she particularly wanted to do outside the suite.

"The sooner I can conclude my meetings with Drake, the sooner we can go home," Daniel added.

He probably thought that was further incentive for her to cooperate. And though she knew it should be, she found herself dreading the conclusion to this adventure.

As much as she detested Drake, as worried as she was about what Daniel was involved in, as concerned as they both were about the not-so-hidden dangers lurking here at the resort, as much as she missed her family, she wasn't looking forward to saying goodbye to Daniel again. This time it would be for good—unless he came to her aunt and uncle's party, an unlikely scenario.

No matter how hard she had tried to resist, she was falling in love with him. Which only served to prove that she was an idiot to fall for a man she didn't even know.

B.J. had never been one to enjoy an afternoon with absolutely nothing to do. Especially when she felt confined by decisions that were not her own.

Flipping discontentedly through the stranger's clothes in her closet, she dressed in the only outfit that seemed to suit her mood. Her own. The green camp shirt and khaki slacks had been laundered and pressed, and she donned them almost defiantly. The momentary surge of rebellion faded as she began to pace restlessly through the empty suite.

She couldn't nap and she had no interest in reading or watching television just then. She wished she knew what was going on in those meetings Daniel had been conducting with Drake for the past three days. It seemed clear that he was setting Drake up for something, but what? A bust? A scam?

It stunned her to think that she had made love twice to the man and she didn't even know whether he was a cop or a criminal.

Wouldn't he have already told her if he was a cop?

Someone tapped on the door. B.J. approached it cautiously, remembering Daniel's warning. She checked the peephole, then frowned. Now this was someone she hadn't expected at all.

"Ingrid?" She opened the door and looked questioningly at the woman on the other side. "This is a surprise."

Looking as fashion-doll perfect as ever in a body-hugging white strapless sundress, Ingrid reached out to clutch B.J.'s shoulder. "Are you all right?"

"Yes, I'm fine, thank you."

"I heard about what happened to you. I can't believe Bernard was so stupid that he left you on the island all night."

"He thought someone else had picked us up," B.J. quoted dutifully.

Ingrid made a scornful sound. "The man is as dumb as a rock. I heard your husband punched him right in the mouth. I wish I had seen that."

"Drake told you that?" B.J. asked in surprise. She hadn't thought Drake was in the habit of sharing gossip with Ingrid.

"Um…no. Someone else told me. Someone who saw it."

The only other person who had witnessed the blow had been the handsome young man who had piloted the boat that collected them from the island. Noting Ingrid's evasive expression, B.J. drew her own conclusions. But all she said was, "I'm sorry I missed your performance last night."

"It wasn't your fault. Though I've got to admit I was pretty ticked off when you weren't there last night. I thought you'd blown me off after you heard my rehearsal."

"No way. I was looking forward to it. How did it go?"

"Pretty good, I think," Ingrid admitted with an un-characteristic lack of hyperbole. "People said some really nice things when I was finished."

"I'm sure you were great. I wish I'd heard you."

"You're nice, you know?" Ingrid smiled, and for a moment B.J. caught a glimpse of how the pretty young Midwesterner might have looked before she'd gotten swept into a world of glamour and jaded wealth.

And then that moment of innocence was gone.

"You want to get out of here?" Ingrid asked, waving a perfectly manicured hand to indicate the suite. Diamonds glittered at her wrist and on her fingers with the movement. "Let's find something to do. Something expensive that we can charge to Judson, since his incompetent staff disappointed both of us last night."

Thinking of Daniel's instructions to stay in the suite, B.J. hesitated, "Oh, I…"

"Come on," Ingrid urged. "It will be fun. You don't want to just sit around all day waiting for your husband, do you?"

B.J. shook her head with a sudden rush of reckless-ness. "No, that isn't what I want to do at all. Let's go."

"Great. Oh, and don't worry about your clothes," In-grid added with a glance at the camp shirt and khakis. "You look fine."

Not even that rather oblivious insult could change B.J.'s mind. Slinging her tote bag over her shoulder, she stepped out of the suite with Ingrid and locked the door behind her.

Chapter Eleven

B.J. and Ingrid spent the entire afternoon being pampered and prettified in the spa and salon. B.J. would have expected to hate every minute of a session like that, being touched and rubbed and fussed over by strangers, but it wasn't so bad.

By the time she and Ingrid parted outside the spa, her skin was soft and glowing, her hair lay in silky layers around her face and her limbs felt fluid and limber. Glancing at her polished fingernails and toenails, she decided she could see herself doing this again—just not anytime soon.

"I'll see you around," Ingrid said, turning in the opposite direction as they left the spa. "It's been fun."

And then she hesitated and said over her shoulder, "It really *has* been fun, B.J. I don't hang out with other women very often, you know?"

"It was nice," B.J. agreed with a smile. She was more accustomed to spending time with women than Ingrid and she couldn't really see Ingrid fitting into her casual circle of friends, but the afternoon had passed quite pleasantly overall. Much better than sitting in the suite all afternoon worrying and waiting for Daniel to return.

In fact, she thought as her steps slowed, she wasn't quite ready yet to go back to the suite. She wasn't eager to face Daniel again with the awareness that she was falling in love with him hanging between them.

She turned abruptly and headed for the beach, avoiding the more populated areas to stroll slowly along a more deserted patch of damp sand. Daniel would probably be annoyed with her for going out by herself like this, but she didn't intend to go far. She simply needed a few minutes alone to fortify herself before seeing him again.

She walked to the edge of the water, letting the waves lap at her toes, unconcerned about her sandals. The breeze blew her freshly trimmed hair around her face. It felt unusually soft and had a light, flowery scent, thanks to whatever products had been used on her. She wondered if Daniel would notice the difference.

And then she grimaced as the thought crossed her mind. She had never been prone to primping for any man, and this was a lousy time to start.

What was she doing, anyway? How could she possibly explain the last four days to anyone else?

That she had allowed herself to be swept into an insane farce of a marriage, that she was helping a man pull off a scam of some sort that he hadn't even bothered to explain for her, that she was falling in love with that man despite having serious doubts about his motives and his moral fiber?

That she was having a no-strings affair with that man—something that was completely out of character for her? That she was fully prepared to make love with him again right now, knowing he wouldn't offer promises or even an assurance that he cared about her—for now or for the future?

Her parents would be certain that she was headed for disaster. Her sister would think she had lost her mind. Her friends would swear she'd been hypnotized into behavior that was completely alien to her. And maybe they would all be right.

But here she was. And she had no intention of leaving until Daniel sent her away.

Brittany Jeanne Samples had changed at some point between climbing out of her rental car outside that Missouri farmhouse and being swept straight into Daniel Andreas's arms. And she sincerely doubted that she would ever be the same again. She only hoped she would somehow find a way to be content with her old life again once she returned to it.

A shell half buried in the sand caught her eye. She bent to pick it up, swishing it a couple of times in the water to clean it.

The shell was a perfectly formed spiral only a couple of inches long, a creamy tan on the outside and soft, gleaming pink inside. Something about it appealed to her. She slipped it into her pocket, intending to take it home as a memento.

Not that she would need any souvenirs to remind her of every minute she had spent with Daniel at this resort. On the contrary, she was afraid that those memories would haunt her for the rest of her life.

"There's a charge for that, you know."

She closed her eyes and stifled a groan before she turned to face Judson Drake. As much as she hated to admit it, she really should have listened to Daniel and gone straight back to the suite.

"B.J.?" Daniel expected to see her sitting in the chair with her book or maybe sprawled in one of the lounge chairs on the balcony, since she seemed to love the ocean air.

It took him only a couple of minutes to determine that she wasn't anywhere in the suite. "Damn it."

It hadn't occurred to him that she would go out despite his request that she stay inside. She had been so cooperative so far, despite her misgivings, that he had taken for granted that she would continue to do as he asked while they were here.

Remembering the spark of defiance in her eyes, he told himself he should have known better.

B.J. was no one's puppet, he reminded himself. She had gone along with him so far because he'd convinced her that it was for her own good, but that didn't

mean she would continue to blindly accept everything
he said.

He remembered the last time she had wandered off
on her own, when she had been followed down the
beach by Bernard. Fortunately she hadn't done anything that time to put herself—or Daniel's cover story—
in jeopardy. His stomach clenched at the possibility
that she might be more reckless this time.

He tried to tell himself it was the plan he was most
worried about, but he knew even as he threw open the
door and headed purposefully out of the suite that his
concerns were all for B.J.

Drake lounged on the beach behind B.J. with his
arms crossed over his chest, his feet planted firmly in
the sand. He was giving her one of those smiles he
probably practiced in front of a mirror—and maybe
some women would be dazzled by its shiny whiteness.
B.J.'s reaction was to want to turn and run.

It was pride as much as responsibility that kept her
where she was. "I beg your pardon?"

"I said there's a charge for taking my shells."

She didn't want to ask what the charge would be. His
smile had just enough leer to it to make her wary. "Perhaps you can bill it to our suite."

He chuckled, the sound so fake it grated on her
nerves. "We'll just consider it my gift to you. You can
think of me when you admire it."

She was in no mood to banter with him. "I take it
your meetings with my husband are over for today.

He'll be looking for me. I should get back to the suite."

Drake didn't move out of her way. "I'm sure he knows you're safe at my resort."

"Funny, I wasn't feeling so safe at one o'clock this morning." The cool remark was a lie, of course. She had felt perfectly safe with Daniel. But she had a role to play—and maybe if she annoyed Drake enough, he'd get out of her way.

"Ah." Drake wasn't notably affected. "You're still annoyed with me about being left on the island. I can't say I blame you for that. It must have been distressing for you to realize that no one was coming for you."

"Yes, it was."

"You must have been terrified."

She lifted her eyebrows. "Inconvenienced, perhaps. A bit nervous. But hardly terrified. After all, I had my husband with me."

"Ah, yes. The overprotective Daniel."

She nodded.

"Your husband is an interesting man. A bit of a hothead."

"He takes good care of me." It was the reply Drake would have expected of her.

"Mmm." He reached out to run a fingertip down her arm. "You're a woman a man would be proud to take care of."

Oh, gag. She managed not to flinch away from his touch, but she could only hope he didn't see the revulsion in her eyes.

Because she knew for a fact that Drake's tastes ran to busty blondes, she didn't take him seriously. Either he was simply in the habit of hitting on every woman who crossed his path or there was something specific he wanted to find out from her. Something about Daniel, maybe.

"I'm about to make your husband a very wealthy man, you know."

Perhaps he wanted to impress her. Make her feel indebted to him. Instead she merely looked bored. "I leave business matters up to Daniel."

"Not impressed, hmm? Wouldn't you like to be dripping with diamonds, B.J.?"

"I have all the diamonds I want. And money to buy more if I choose," she added, keeping her so-called fortune in mind. "If Daniel wants the satisfaction of making more money on his own, then I fully support him in his efforts."

"You aren't into flash, are you? Simple clothes, tasteful jewelry, a plain gold wedding ring. I'd have bought you something much more spectacular if I'd married you. Just to show everyone how proud I was to have you for my bride."

B.J. instinctively rubbed her thumb over the wedding band on her ring finger. "This ring has deep sentimental value for my husband and for me. It's all I want. Now if you'll excuse me, I'd better—"

Drake stroked her arm again. "You're very loyal to your husband. Perhaps rather foolishly so."

She bit her lip and remained silent.

He took a step closer to her, making her balance her weight on both feet in preparation, should he make it necessary for her to strike out or run. "I don't suppose there would be any point in asking if you'd like to have dinner with me sometime. In Paris, perhaps."

"My wife and I would be delighted to join you in Paris for dinner sometime." Daniel's voice was as smooth as glass as he stepped from behind Drake to slide an arm around B.J.'s shoulders and draw her away from the other man. "Wouldn't we, darling?"

She looked up at him in relief. "I'd have to check my calendar, of course."

Daniel smiled and pressed a light kiss on her nose. "My wife and her social calendar," he said indulgently. "That's only one of the little things I love about her."

Drake's smile was decidedly forced now. "Daniel. Nice to see you. Will you be joining me for dinner this evening?"

B.J. held her breath until Daniel shook his head. His arm tightened around her, and his voice had dropped half an octave when he replied, "Thank you, but B.J. and I have plans for this evening. It's an anniversary for us, and we'd like to commemorate it privately."

"This is your wedding anniversary?" Drake asked somewhat skeptically.

"No." Daniel gazed into B.J.'s eyes, giving her a very private smile. "It's another sort. One we like to celebrate in our own way."

She felt her cheeks go red, which probably only strengthened the act Daniel was putting on for Drake's benefit. Something about the way Daniel was looking at made her knees soften. It wasn't hard to fill in the blanks of the "special anniversary" he was making up for them.

Apparently Drake had filled in a few blanks of his own. Looking as though he had bitten into something sour, he nodded. "Then I'll see you first thing tomorrow to sign the papers. This time tomorrow you'll have something to celebrate again."

"Tomorrow?" B.J. spun to face Daniel as soon as Drake left them alone. "We're going to have to stay another night?"

"Just one more," he replied, studying her flushed face. "I promise."

"That's what you told me yesterday."

"I got us out of having dinner with Creepy Guy," he said hopefully.

She refused to smile. "By implying that we're going to spend the evening in bed?"

"Sorry. It was the first excuse that occurred to me."

He didn't look at all sorry.

"Do you know how worried my family must be about me? I've never in my life taken this much time away without telling anyone where I am."

"So maybe now they'll see you as all grown-up, rather than the baby sister. They'll treat you with more respect."

"You spin everything to suit your purposes, don't you?"

"Isn't that what a good con man always does?"

The humor in his voice had turned dark, and it brought a lump to her throat rather than making her smile. "Apparently."

He lifted a hand to her hair, brushing his fingers across the newly trimmed edges. "You got your hair cut."

"Yes."

"Looks good. And you're wearing pink polish on your fingers and your toes."

She should have known he would notice everything. Her toes curled self-consciously in her sandals. "Ingrid and I spent a couple of hours at the spa this afternoon. It was my way of making up to her for missing her performance last night."

"You look very nice." Still holding her in one arm, he turned to sniff appreciatively at her softly scented hair. "Smell good, too."

"Aren't you going to chew me out for leaving the suite after you advised me not to?"

"There was no harm in going to the spa. As for walking on the beach alone—" he shrugged against her "—judging by the look on your face when I found you with Drake, I think my point was made without me having to say I told you so."

She sighed. "I suppose you're right. I was *so* glad to see you."

He turned her to face him. "Show me."

Was this another performance? Did Daniel think Drake was still lurking around, watching them? Bernard, maybe?

Aware of those possible onlookers, she lifted her

face to his. She was still vaguely annoyed with him, still worried about the outcome of all this role-playing…but she couldn't seem to miss any opportunity to kiss him.

The scent that had been sprayed on B.J. smelled sultry and expensive, and Daniel liked it on her. But then, he was turned on by the scent of plain soap on her soft, supple skin, he had to admit. Everything about her appealed to him, and it had nothing to do with any artifice slathered on from a jar.

Even after everything she had gone through because of him, she still kissed him with a sweetness and eagerness that nearly brought him to his knees.

She fit so perfectly into his arms. Felt so very right against him.

A surge of possessiveness coursed through him, making his hold on her tighten and his mouth move more roughly over hers. He could still see Drake standing next to her, putting his sleazy hands on her, bringing a look of wariness to her eyes.

His first impulse had been violent. Murderous. Only the realization that he would have been putting B.J. in even more danger had given him the strength to push the anger back and use his brains instead of his fists.

He lifted his head, gasping for breath. If he were to have his way, they would make love right now, right here on the sand. They would let the surf wash over them, as in that old movie, and forget about Drake and the past and the future and anything but each other.

Because it was the middle of the afternoon and there

was a chance that someone could stroll by at any minute, he forced himself to take a few deep breaths. "Let's go back to the suite."

Her blue eyes were darker than usual, the expression in them hard to read when she gazed up at him. They were pressed too closely together for her to be unaware of how badly he wanted her. She knew exactly why he was in a hurry to get back to the suite.

He could offer her nothing except a few hours of pleasure. And he knew full well it wasn't her usual style to settle for that.

She deserved so much more.

And then she smiled up at him and took his hand. "All right."

He found himself oddly unable to speak, his throat suddenly so tight he almost choked. He turned with her toward the path that led to their suite. Their bed.

"Wait."

B.J. stopped and reached into her pocket. He watched as she pulled out a little shell and threw it into the water. And then she turned back to him and took his hand again. "Now I'm ready."

He didn't know what had just happened, but as she slipped an arm around his waist and matched her steps to his, he found he couldn't really care.

Maybe he would remember to ask her later.

"Daniel?"

He stirred against her, his face cloaked in the early-evening shadows that darkened the bedroom. His voice sounded groggy. Utterly sated. "Hmm?"

She squirmed onto her right side and rested her weight on her arm, touching his face with her left hand. "You need a shave."

He chuckled lazily. "That's what you wanted to tell me?"

"No. Just a momentary distraction." There were so many distracting things about Daniel, especially when he was lying naked in the tangled sheets, his chest still glistening with dampness from their exertion.

"Mmm." He seemed to be getting distracted again himself, as his right hand slid up her rib cage toward her breast.

"Wait. I want to ask you something."

What might have been a slight grimace crossed his face, but his tone was light when he said, "Just as well. I'm not sure I've got the energy for anything else. At the moment, anyway."

"You're scared to death of what I'm going to ask you, aren't you?" she asked in exasperation.

"Not scared. Just…cautious."

It would serve him right if she asked something she knew he wouldn't want to answer—like exactly what was going on between him and Drake. Instead she said simply, "When are we going to eat? I'm starving."

He lay very still for a moment and then he laughed. His laughter was deep, rich, pleasant—and it made her chest ache because she had heard the sound so very rarely. She knew she would always treasure the echo of it.

* * *

They dined under the stars at a table for two set far enough away from the other diners that it was obvious they wanted to be alone. They sat with their heads close together, enjoying the food and wine, sharing bites, grinning foolishly at each other.

They didn't talk much—there wasn't much they could say within the parameters of safe topics Daniel had set for them—but B.J. enjoyed every minute of the meal anyway. She knew Daniel was acting out the story he'd told Drake earlier about them celebrating a private "special anniversary," but she didn't care. The night was magical.

She'd worn one of the pretty sundresses. The diamond bracelet glittered on her wrist and the borrowed gold ring gleamed on her left hand.

Daniel wore a summer-weight jacket and a tie, and he looked like any woman's daydream of the perfect dinner companion. When he held her hand across the table, his own wedding band reflected the multicolored party lights strung above them.

It was so easy to pretend it was all real. So tempting to lose herself in the fantasy, even though she knew it was foolish. Even though she had no doubt she would be devastated when it ended.

They moved to the dance floor when they'd finished their meals. The band obliged their mood by playing blatantly romantic music that allowed them to sway together, arms entangled, his cheek pressed to her hair.

It was the kind of evening that B.J. had experienced

only in books and romantic movies before. The kind she
had never really expected to experience herself.

As Daniel's lips brushed the side of her face and his
hands slid down her back to rest intimately at her hips,
she knew she would remember every moment of this
evening for the rest of her life. She only hoped she
could recall only the pleasure and not the inevitable
pain.

Whatever the outcome, she thought as he pressed a
kiss at the corner of her mouth, she could never regret
this night. For just a few hours she had been someone
different, someone sophisticated and interesting. A
woman in love with a fascinating, extraordinary man.
A woman who was wanted by that same uncommon
man in return.

The music ended and they moved a couple of inches
apart to politely applaud. Someone said her name from
nearby, and B.J. glanced around to see Kurt McGuire
from Tulsa standing a few feet away, his arm around a
pretty, slightly plump redhead.

She smiled and nodded to them, then turned back to
Daniel, who was frowning at Kurt in a way that had the
other man turning hastily away again. "Stop that. You're
intimidating him."

"Good. I intended to."

She sighed and shook her head. "You're incorrigible."

"Hmm." He wrapped his arms around her and drew
her close to him again, seemingly oblivious to anyone
who might be looking on—but then, B.J. knew better.
"Come back to the suite and I'll show you incorrigible."

Her eyebrows rose as she slipped her arms around his neck. "I thought you were all out of energy?"

His smile was downright piratical. "I seem to have recovered."

Feeling the hard ridge against her thigh, she blinked in astonishment. "I guess you have."

His smile faded. "Come back to the suite, B.J. We have a few more hours together. Let's make the most of them."

Her heart twisted at the candid reminder that their time was running out—but like Daniel, she was reluctant to waste another minute.

She took his hand and let him lead her off the dance floor.

"There's only one thing I want you to promise me," she whispered as Daniel lowered her to the bed.

Though his lips were already at her throat, she felt him stiffen—and it hurt that he seemed to have braced himself for whatever she was going to ask. "What?"

"Just tell me this isn't casual for you. Even if it's only for tonight."

"B.J." He cupped her face in his hands and stared almost fiercely into her eyes. "It isn't casual. It would be so much easier if it were."

There was no mistaking the truth in his eyes. He was a good actor, but surely no one could be *that* good.

"That's all I wanted to know," she murmured and pulled him down into her arms.

For now.

Chapter Twelve

B.J. should have been sleepy, but she found herself wide-awake an hour after they returned to the suite. They'd made love, and though it was hard to believe it could keep getting better, somehow it did. Something told her a lifetime of lovemaking with Daniel would never grow old—

But that was something she would never know, she told herself glumly.

Which reminded her… "Daniel?"

"Are you hungry *again?*" he asked in feigned dismay.

She chuckled obligingly, then grew serious again. "Those papers Drake said you were signing tomorrow? That's what you've been working toward this week?"

She could see his face well enough in the shadows to watch his relaxed expression go hard and guarded. A little part of her heart broke at this latest demonstration that the closeness between them ended at the bedroom door.

"Yes," he said without further elaboration.

"And then what?"

"I move on. Fairly quickly."

Taking his money and running from Drake? "Where will you go?"

"Somewhere a long way from Drake. By this time tomorrow he's going to be…displeased with me. He'll have figured out that he's been taken for a very expensive ride."

She moistened her suddenly dry lips with the tip of her tongue. "And what about me?"

"You'll be safe. I have a plan to get you away as I leave."

Focusing very hard on her questions rather than her pain, she looked at her hand where it rested on his chest. The borrowed gold band on her finger was just visible in the shadows, but she felt its weight as her hand pressed against his steadily beating heart. "Will *you* be safe?"

His silence was an ominous reply in itself.

"Will I ever see you again?" Though she spoke in a whisper, she knew he heard her.

The fact that he didn't answer broke what remained of her heart.

"What did you expect, B.J.?" he asked roughly after a long, painful few moments. "I've told you what I am. What kind of life I live. There's no place for you in it."

It was amazing how a heart that was already broken could still shatter further.

Fool, she told herself angrily, blinking away tears. *You knew this was coming.*

Which didn't make it hurt any less.

Keeping her face averted from him, she tossed off the sheets and reached for her robe. "I think I'll take a shower. I feel a little…grubby."

He made a move as if to detain her, made a sound that might have been the beginning of her name. But then he went still. "Save some hot water for me," was all he said.

Maybe he was feeling grubby, too.

Her legs were somewhat rubbery when she stood, but she thought she could make it to the shower. Just.

Closing the bathroom door behind her, she crossed the spacious granite floor and reached into the glass-enclosed shower stall to turn on the water. She didn't step in immediately, taking a moment to bury her face in her hands and get her emotions under control—at least, as much as possible just then. She refused to allow herself to fall apart in front of Daniel, no matter what might happen between them next.

She would save her tears for after they said goodbye.

Daniel looked at the closed bathroom door for a long time, and then he shoved himself from the rumpled bed and began to pace in long, furious strides. He would have liked to have thrown something, smashed something fragile and expensive against the elegant walls of this oppressively lavish suite, but that would have brought B.J. running to find out what was going on. And he wanted a few minutes away from her.

Damn it, he didn't need this. Hadn't asked for this. He'd been operating just fine on his own, without anyone special in his life. A man with no past, no future, only a grim determination to achieve his goals and move on victorious to the next challenge.

B.J. made him feel too much. Want too much. Regret too many of the decisions he had made during the past few years.

She was so good. So kindhearted. She should never have been tainted by her association with him. She deserved a hell of a lot more than he could ever offer her. He wouldn't invite any woman into the darkness of his life—especially B.J., who belonged irrevocably in the light.

He had to send her back to Texas, back to the family who loved her and protected her, the parents and siblings and aunts and uncles and cousins who would all want more for her than the likes of him. He had never belonged in that circle, never been more than a generously welcomed outsider. He had known that the first time he'd seen her among them. He had known it the first time he had kissed her. And he had known it the first time he'd told her goodbye—a parting he had always believed would be permanent.

He wished it had been permanent. It would have been so much safer for her...and God knew it would have been a lot less painful for him.

Throwing on a robe, he reached into his bag and

drew out a cell phone. The shower was still running, so he figured he had a few minutes of privacy.

It was time that he did something productive with those stolen minutes, before everything he had worked so hard for fell apart around him.

Drawing a deep breath, B.J. dropped her hands and reached for the tie on her robe, intending to step into the now-steaming shower. Only then did she realize that she had forgotten her nightgown.

She sighed again. For some reason, she found herself reluctant to dress in front of Daniel. She would rather emerge from the bathroom with her dignity intact—and herself fully clothed.

Leaving the shower running—Daniel could worry about his own hot water—she stepped into the bedroom, finding it empty and the door to the sitting room ajar. She frowned when she heard the low rumble of Daniel's voice from the other room.

Who was he talking to? Surely Drake hadn't come by even after Daniel had made it clear they didn't want to be disturbed tonight.

She didn't want to be seen by whoever it was, but she was too curious not to at least take a peek. Keeping to one side of the doorway, she moved closer, trying to see into the other room.

Daniel was alone, it turned out. He had his back to her and he was talking into a cell phone. Something about his tone told her he didn't want to be overheard—which, of course, only made her listen harder.

"I want her out of here tomorrow," he said, sounding as if he would tolerate no argument. "First thing."

B.J. bit her lower lip, realizing that he must be talking about her. She leaned closer to the doorway.

"No, I don't care about the details, just get her out of here before she ruins everything. The longer she stays, the more chance there is she's going to make a wrong move. We're too close to the payoff to risk that."

It didn't sound as if he was worried about her as much as his mysterious plan. Which made her irrationally indignant.

How could he act as if she was such a liability? Hadn't she cooperated with everything he had asked? Hadn't she gone beyond what should have been expected of her to convince Drake and the others that she was exactly who Daniel had said she was?

"Yeah, she's asking questions. But I've managed to distract her. For now."

She scowled. He had certainly kept her distracted. It devastated her to think that their lovemaking had been his way of keeping her too occupied to ask questions. He has assured her it wasn't casual—but maybe they defined the term in drastically different ways.

"Look, just take care of her, okay? I'm trusting you to handle this."

Take care of her. There were several ways to interpret that, B.J. thought as she hurried silently back to the bathroom, closed the door without a sound, then ducked into the steamy shower.

Considering the hardness of Daniel's voice and the

harshness of his words, some people might be frightened at this point. At the very least, concerned for their safety.

Perhaps it was just further evidence of B.J.'s idiocy where Daniel was concerned that she had no fear of him at all. Maybe she couldn't trust him with her heart, but she trusted him with her life. He had promised she would leave this resort safely, and she believed him.

Some people might consider her less than intelligent to place her faith in the word of an admitted con man. Or accuse her of once again confusing the past with the present.

All she could say in reply was that she believed instinctively that neither the Daniel she had known then nor the man she knew now would do anything to harm her physically. Nor would he allow anyone else to do so.

She wasn't romanticizing him, she promised herself. She didn't try to delude herself that any of his actions here were noble or selfless. He had told her he was here for the money, and she believed him. But she could never be afraid of him.

"B.J.? You okay in there?"

Realizing that the shower had been running for quite a long time, she hastily shut it off, scooping wet hair away from her face. "I'll be right out."

Daniel woke her with a soft kiss pressed against her lips. Blinking groggily, she realized that it was barely daylight outside, with hardly enough light to filter through the sheer draperies. She didn't remember finally drifting off to sleep.

She could just see his face when she peered up at him. She noted immediately that he was fully dressed, sitting on the side of the bed, gazing down at her.

"What is it? Where are you going?"

"I have to go out. There's something I need to tell you first."

She was suddenly completely awake. The phone call she had overheard the night before came back to her now, giving her a sick certainty that what he needed to say was goodbye.

"This is it, isn't it?"

He didn't seem surprised by her question. She'd like to think he looked a bit saddened by it. "Yes."

She swallowed and asked simply, "What do you want me to do?"

He touched her face. "That's all you're going to ask?"

"Would you answer me if I asked more?"

His mouth quirked in what might have been an attempt at a smile. "Probably not."

"That's what I thought."

He leaned over to kiss her again. "Thank you for making it easier."

"You still owe me," she whispered.

He rested his forehead against hers for a moment. "I know."

And then he straightened, speaking more briskly. "I've got to go. Someone will be here soon—someone who'll take you to safety. I want you to go straight back to Dallas the minute you get the chance. Promise me that."

"I promise."

She saw his shoulders relax and knew that she had just set his mind at ease. Apparently he trusted her word as much as she trusted his.

He would never have to know how much that promise had cost her. How much she wanted to beg him to let her stay with him.

It was partly because she was afraid she would put him in danger if she remained that she agreed to leave. And partly because she couldn't bear it if he told her that he wasn't even tempted to ask her to stay.

Holding the sheets to her chest, she rose on one elbow to watch him walk toward the bedroom doorway. Already she saw him taking on the tough, hardened persona of the man Judson Drake knew as Daniel Andreas. It was something in the way he walked, the way he carried himself.

"Daniel?"

He paused in the doorway, looking over his shoulder, impatience in his eyes. But his voice was still indulgent when he asked, "What is it?"

"I just want you to know I'm in love with you."

She had the minor satisfaction of seeing his impressive control slip then and knowing she had done something few people ever could. She had caught Daniel Andreas completely off guard. "B.J., I—"

"Go play your power games, Daniel," she said

gently. "I'm not asking you for anything. I just needed to say it one time out loud."

He'd gotten his expression back under control now. His white-knuckle grip on the doorjamb was the only sign that he was still reeling from her admission. "Take care of yourself, B.J."

"You do the same."

He drew a deep, painful-sounding breath. "I always have," he said. And then he was gone.

Hearing the sitting room door close behind him, B.J. finally gave in to the tears she had refused to shed in front of him.

Though they were wrinkled from wearing them a few hours the day before, B.J. donned her own clothes again. Nothing went into her tote bag except the things she had brought with her; she wanted nothing that came from Drake's resort.

It was so quiet in the rooms with Daniel gone. It felt oddly as though they were already unoccupied, despite the clothes that hung in the closets and the other personal items scattered around.

She could almost hear the echo of her declaration of love hanging in the still air.

It still amazed her that she had found the courage to say those words to Daniel. Because she hadn't expected to hear them in return, it hadn't hurt—at least, not too badly—that he'd left without commenting on them.

She wasn't sorry that she had told him. Daniel hadn't been given nearly enough love in his lifetime. Just once she had wanted him to know that sometimes love came as a gift, without any expectations or encumbrances. And even if he didn't feel it in return, maybe it would mean something to him someday that she had found him worthy of her love.

Someone knocked at the door just as she was finishing buttoning her shirt. Daniel certainly hadn't given her much warning, she thought with a pang in her heart.

Carrying her tote bag with her, she crossed the sitting room and opened the door. A stocky-looking man in the resort service uniform stood on the other side. Not exactly what she'd been expecting. "Yes?"

"Mrs. Andreas?"

She nodded. Staying in character until the end, she thought ironically.

"Your husband asked me to come for you. He and Mr. Drake would like for you to join them for breakfast."

She frowned, confused. Daniel hadn't said anything about breakfast. But he had said someone would be coming for her. Maybe this was a cover story, in case anyone was watching her or something. "I, um—"

The man held the door open more widely. "They're expecting you," he prodded.

She glanced over her shoulder, saying a brief good-bye to the overly fussy suite—and to the man with whom she had shared it. "All right. I'm ready."

She took great pride in the fact that her voice was steady despite the flood of emotions pouring through her.

Her escort smiled as he closed the door behind them.

Something about that smile sent an odd feeling shoot-
ing through her, but she told herself she was being
paranoid. She trusted Daniel, she reminded herself. He
wouldn't send anyone for her who posed any threat
to her.

Holding her head high, she allowed the uniformed
man to lead her down the hallway.

Daniel was having a great deal of trouble concentrating on what he was supposed to be doing. Though
Drake was droning on about something or other that
should be of interest, Daniel heard an entirely different
voice instead. Entirely different words.

I just want you to know I'm in love with you.

His fists clenched beneath the table. What on earth
could make her think he deserved a gift like that?

It wouldn't last, of course. It wasn't real. She'd been
affected by the romance of the evening before, dazzled
by their lovemaking.

Maybe it was transference or one of those other psy-
chological phenomena that supposedly happened when
someone found herself swept into a bizarre situation
and had only one ally to turn to. Or maybe it was just
the memory of a troubled young boy who no longer ex-
isted and a restless young girl who had felt stifled by
the expectations of her huge, loving family.

She would come to her senses as soon as she was
safely back in her real life. It wasn't love. But for just
a little while it had felt an awful lot like it.

"You're drifting again, Daniel. Having trouble paying attention this morning?"

Drake looked sleazier than usual when Daniel glanced across the table. Maybe it was just the contrast to the purity of the images in his mind. "Go on. I'm listening."

Drake tented his fingers and studied Daniel coolly over them. "You know, I've always paid attention to my instincts. They've kept me out of more trouble than you can imagine over the years."

Daniel lifted an eyebrow. "I'm sure they have." He had great respect for Drake's instincts himself, which was why he had been so careful around him.

"Yes, well, lately I've been getting a few signals from you that have bothered me. So I've taken steps to make sure that I have your full cooperation as we conclude our business."

The small hairs on the back of Daniel's neck seemed to stand suddenly on end. "What are you talking about?"

"I've been watching you with your wife during the past few days. It's been…an enlightening experience for me."

Every muscle in his body going tense, Daniel remained silent, staring at the other man with narrowed eyes.

Drake's smile had turned rather pitying. "You misled me about her, you know."

Oh, hell. "In what way?"

"You implied that you married her for her money. That you've been humoring her so she wouldn't ask many questions about your dealings with her holdings."

Daniel forced himself to shrug carelessly, relieved that Drake was still buying the marriage charade. "That's the truth, basically. I keep her happy and she asks nothing more of me."

"But it's not entirely the truth. You didn't add that you're in love with your wife."

Daniel snorted—and the incredulous reaction wasn't entirely feigned. "Get real, Drake."

"Oh, I am real. I'm not the sort of man to develop special feelings for any particular woman, of course, but I like to consider myself a shrewd judge of other men's weaknesses. Brittany is your weakness. You wouldn't do anything to put her at risk."

B.J. was safe, Daniel reminded himself. He had seen to that. Which didn't mean he had to like the way this jerk was talking about her. "I have no intention of putting my wife at risk. Now if we could get back to—"

"She wasn't what I expected, you know. I would have thought you'd be more attracted to someone like Ingrid. Beautiful. Built. Sophisticated. I didn't think you would have fallen for someone who looks barely old enough to be out of school, with no figure to speak of and too much naiveté to be particularly interesting."

Daniel's fists tightened at the dismissive—and so very inadequate—summary of B.J.'s charms. "Yes, well, there's no accounting for taste," he managed to say lightly. "Especially when there's enough money involved."

"Mmm. I found your devotion to your bride heart-warming. And quite useful. It never occurred to me before that she could be a very handy tool for me to insure that you would give me no problems during our…negotiations."

Daniel grunted impatiently. "My wife has nothing to do with our business. And I've given you no reason to distrust me. You don't need to convince me to cooperate—I've been doing so all along. So let's get on with it."

"But you see, I'm the type of man who takes advantage of every fortuitous development when it comes to business," Drake murmured. "The trait has been very useful to me in the past. And I think you should know that I've arranged a little insurance so that you won't try to pull off anything foolish as we conclude our dealings. I'm sure you had no such scheme in mind, but just in case…"

"What the hell are you talking about, Drake?"

"Your wife, of course. Don't worry, she's perfectly safe. And she'll remain that way as long as you continue to cooperate. Once I've been assured that everything is proceeding as planned, you will be reunited with her."

Daniel started to rise. "What have you done?"

"You'll want to sit back down, Mr. Andreas," Bernard advised from his usual position at the back of Drake's conference room. His hand was already inside his jacket.

A squarely built man with cold eyes and a hard smile tapped on the door and entered the room just then. "Everything's secured, Mr. Drake."

"Thank you, Paul." Drake looked at Daniel with an unmistakable look of self-satisfaction. "Paul has taken your wife to a safe location. At least, safe for now. So…with that out of the way, shall we proceed?"

A surge of hatred coursed through Daniel with enough force to leave him momentarily speechless. Hatred for Drake, who had dared to threaten B.J. And for himself, for putting her in this position in the first place.

He had been so careless. So arrogant. So insufferably certain that he had taken every step to keep her safe, even as he had used her as ruthlessly as Drake was doing now. She had made a handy accomplice in his cover—and she had played her part so convincingly that Drake had bought it even more convincingly than Daniel had predicted he would.

He should have foreseen what Drake would do if a convenient innocent crossed his path.

"Damn you, Drake, what have you done with her?" he demanded in a roar, surging out of his chair with a reckless disregard for Bernard and his ever-present weapon. *"Where is my wife?"*

It took both Bernard and the newcomer to wrestle Daniel back into his chair.

Drake simply looked on with cool amusement. He ended the struggle with a few well-selected words. "I said she would be safe as long as you cooperate, Daniel. I would hardly call this cooperation."

Daniel went still in the chair.

"Much better," Drake assured him, nodding to his employees to release him. They did so but remained poised close by.

Drake reached for the file in front of him again, as

though they were still engaged in business as usual. "Shall we get back to it? And by the way, Daniel, you would really be wasting your breath to try to convince me again that you aren't in love with B.J. It's really very touching, isn't it, Bernard?"

Bernard laughed.

Chapter Thirteen

"Stupid. Stupid, stupid, *stupid!*" With each muttered word, B.J. hit herself in the forehead. The last time she hit hard enough to make her ears ring a little, but she didn't care. She had never been angrier with herself.

She couldn't believe she had just blithely walked into a trap. Hadn't even considered the possibility that she should be on her guard. Daniel had told her he was sending someone for her, and she had just naively followed the first guy who'd come along.

The man she'd assumed had been sent by Daniel had instead locked her in a storage room. According to her watch almost half an hour had passed since, though it felt like much longer.

Glaring at the cases of toilet paper, facial tissues and paper towels stacked around her, she kicked the locked door. The only thing that accomplished was to hurt her big toe, which was left unprotected by her sandals. Cursing herself again, she hobbled furiously around the roughly eight-by-eight room, trying to come up with a plan for escape.

Since she couldn't figure out any way to break through a solidly bolted door with a roll of toilet paper, she sank to the floor and rested her forehead on her up-drawn knees. She didn't know why she was here. The man who had pushed her inside and locked the door behind her hadn't stayed around long enough to answer any questions.

She couldn't help remembering the things she had overheard Daniel saying into his cell phone the night before. He had told someone to get her out of the way—and he'd added that he didn't really care about the details.

Was this his idea of keeping her safe? Out of the way?

If so, why hadn't he just locked her in the suite? Or told her not to leave. After her encounter with Drake on the beach yesterday, he must have known she wouldn't be in any hurry to go out by herself again.

No. There was something else going on here. She really didn't think the man who had locked her in this room had been working with Daniel at all. She would be willing to bet everything that he was one of Drake's men.

Which meant that Daniel didn't know where she

was. He would be worried about her—and that meant he couldn't concentrate on whatever he was doing with Drake. Which, she thought with a sinking feeling, was probably the whole point.

Drake must have figured out—or at least suspected—that Daniel wasn't being entirely up front with him in their shady dealings. Was grabbing her his way of ensuring Daniel's cooperation? If so, they had done a good job of convincing everyone they were really married.

And *she,* B.J. thought with a groan, must have done a very good job of making everyone believe she wasn't very bright. That she would simply walk into a storage closet if someone told her to.

"Stupid, *stupid!*"

She wouldn't entirely blame herself. Daniel should have told her who to expect. Given her some sort of password or something. He knew Drake better than she did; he should have expected an underhanded move like this from Creepy Guy.

But she was the one who had gotten herself locked in a closet, she thought with another low groan.

The door rattled, and B.J. jumped to her feet, braced for trouble. She'd had some lessons in self-defense; she would fight if she had to.

"B.J." Ingrid peeked cautiously into the room. "Are you in here?"

B.J. rushed toward the door. "Ingrid? Yes! I'm here."

Ingrid stepped inside the storeroom, leaving the door ajar behind her. "I thought it was really weird when I saw Paul leading you into the back hallways of the building. I started following—because I'm just nosy sometimes, but I had this feeling I needed to know what was going on. Then when Paul pushed you in here and locked the door, I ducked out of sight and waited for him to go away. I'm sorry, but it took me a while to find a key to let you out."

"Oh, Ingrid, thank you." She spontaneously hugged her.

"I couldn't believe what he did," Ingrid said indignantly. "I know Judson was behind it. I'm sure he was flexing his muscles around your husband. Judson gets off on power, you know—and if he thought he could get something more from Daniel by snatching you, he wouldn't even hesitate."

B.J. would have liked to ask why Ingrid would sleep with the man when she knew so many bad things about him, but that was really none of her business. Maybe Ingrid would demand better for herself from now on— at least, B.J. hoped so. In the meantime, she needed to find a way to let Daniel know she was all right.

"I must find my husband," she said, moving toward the door. It occurred to her that it grew easier all the time to refer to him that way.

Ingrid caught her arm. "Wait."

Impatiently B.J. tried to shake her off. "But I have to—"

"B.J., something's going on out there. I saw some things when I was looking for a key."

"What did you see?"

Ingrid spoke in an urgent whisper. "I think there's been a raid or something. Cops, you know? I saw Bernard in handcuffs, being shoved into a big, dark car. I'm—I'm really sorry, B.J., but I think Judson and Daniel are in trouble."

B.J.'s head was starting to pound. "We need to go find out what's going on."

"Oh, I, uh—"

Seeing the trepidation in Ingrid's expression, B.J. sighed. "Okay. I'll go see what's going on. You go back to your room and pack. If Drake's been arrested, you'll probably want to leave the resort rather quickly. I assume you have someplace to go?"

"Oh, sure. I've got a nice apartment in L.A."

B.J. wouldn't ask how Ingrid afforded a nice place in Los Angeles. "Fine. Make a good life for yourself, Ingrid. And thank you again for letting me out."

"Yeah, sure. I owed you, you know? Maybe we'll see each other again sometime?"

"Maybe we will." With a quick smile, B.J. turned and hurried down the hallway that led past a laundry room—the same hallway through which she had obligingly followed Paul earlier.

It was an indication of how meticulously Drake's employees had been trained that there was little pandemonium at the resort even through the boss had been led away in handcuffs. B.J. heard people talking about the scandal as soon as she reached the lobby of the main lodge, but the staff seemed to be carrying on with their responsibilities, if only because they didn't know what else to do.

She headed for the front desk, intending to ask if anyone knew anything about Daniel. A hand on her shoulder stopped her in her tracks.

It took her a moment to recognize the dark-haired young man who stood behind her. And then she remembered. "You're Greg, right? From the boat."

He nodded, looking relieved. "I have a message for you. From Daniel."

B.J. clutched his arm. "Daniel? Where is he? Is he okay?"

"Hang on just a minute." Greg flipped open a cell phone, pressed a button and held it to his ear. "I've got her," he said a moment later. "She looks fine."

B.J.'s fingers tightened on his sleeve. "Is that Daniel? Can I talk to him?"

He shook his head. "Yeah, I'll tell her," he said into the phone.

B.J. stared numbly at him as he closed the phone and slipped it into his pocket. "Where is he?"

"He had to leave," Greg replied. "I've been instructed to make sure you get on a plane back to Texas."

"I don't understand. Daniel *left?*" Just like that? Without a goodbye or anything?

"Well, he's gone now. He was waiting to make sure you were safe."

Across the lobby, two men wearing dark suits and carrying walkie-talkies entered an elevator and disappeared. A search of the premises? Were they looking for Daniel?

"I don't know what's going on," she said and she knew she sounded bewildered.

Greg patted her arm, his expression sympathetic. "I'm just glad you're okay. I was delayed on my way to collect you this morning and by the time I arrived at the suite you were gone. I was searching the grounds for you when the feds arrived and things got sort of chaotic around here. I ran into Ingrid on the way to her suite. She told me you were safe. I contacted Daniel immediately. I've got to tell you, he just about went crazy when we didn't know where you were."

B.J. bit her lip, keeping her reaction to herself.

"Anyway, he wanted me to tell you that he's sorry Drake tried to put you in the middle. Daniel's really angry with himself for not anticipating that."

"Just what's your connection to Daniel, anyway?" She was getting irritable enough to picture him as a dummy sitting on Daniel's knee and spouting Daniel's words, but it would just take too much energy to be that snide with him at the moment. The ups and downs of the morning had drained all the fight out of her. For now.

Greg shrugged. "He asked me to do him a couple of favors and he promised me a few in return."

Obviously Greg wasn't going to be any more informative than Daniel had been. Still, she tried. "Where is he?"

"In all the uproar, he managed to slip away just as the feds arrived."

"And what would have happened to him if he had stayed?" she demanded, staring fiercely into Greg's unrevealing dark eyes.

He only shrugged.

"You know how to call him. Will you call him now? I want to talk to him."

"He wouldn't answer," Greg said, his voice gentle now, a note of sympathy in it that made her shoulders straighten. "Now that he knows you're safe, he's probably turned off the phone."

She wouldn't ask anything else of him, she vowed. If there was one thing she did not need, it was this guy's pity.

"Fine," she said shortly. "I want to go home now."

Greg nodded. "It will be safe to go back up to your suite now, if you'd like to pack. Daniel told me to be sure you take everything with you."

All the clothes Daniel—or someone—had provided for her during her stay here. She shook her head. "There's nothing in the suite that I want."

"You're sure?"

"Positive."

"Oh, that reminds me." He reached into his pocket and drew out two items that he pressed into her hand. "These are yours, I think."

She glanced at her wallet and her cell phone, then stuffed them into her tote. Now she was leaving with everything she'd brought with her, she thought. Everything except her heart.

Greg waved a hand toward the exits. "Okay, let's see about getting you on your way—"

"B.J.? Are you okay?"

The sound of her name made her turn to face the man who crossed the lobby toward her looking both worried and relieved. A tall, slender man in his early fifties, his dark hair was lightly frosted with gray, and his left eyebrow was neatly bisected by an old, thin white scar.

Had she not been clinging so very tightly to the tattered remains of her pride, she might well have burst into tears at the sight of him. As it was, she walked into his arms and rested her cheek tightly against his reassuringly solid chest. "Uncle Ryan."

"Do you know how worried we've been about you? Your mother's about ready to call out the National Guard."

"How did you find me? No, never mind. I don't care. And I'm not even really surprised. I'm just glad to see you."

Her mother's brother tilted her face up to his, studying her with concerned eyes. "You're all right?"

"I'm fine," she assured him. Physically, it was the truth. Emotionally…well, she would be fine, she promised herself. Eventually.

"What's going on here, anyway?"

B.J. looked over her shoulder, wondering if Greg would be more willing to answer questions for her uncle than he had been for her. But he hadn't waited around to be questioned by either one of them. He was no longer standing where he had been only moments before, nor anywhere else in the lobby, as far as she could see.

"I'll tell you what I know on the way home," she said

to her uncle, drawing away from him. "Let's just get out of here now, okay?"

"Have you got everything you're taking with you?"

She hugged her tote more tightly against her. "There's nothing left for me here," she murmured and turned toward the exit.

Apparently sensing that B.J. wasn't in the mood to talk, Ryan didn't push her for answers or conversation during the long flight back to Dallas. He had arrived in the private jet that belonged to D'Alessandro and Walker Investigations, so they had plenty of room to stretch out and be comfortable.

B.J. stared out the window, watching the ground passing beneath them, wondering if they had flown over Daniel.

Shouldn't she be feeling more like herself now, as they drew ever closer to home? She had on her own clothes, sat with the uncle who had known her since she was barely more than a toddler, was headed back to the extensive family who knew her and loved her.

So why did she still feel so very different from the woman who had left Dallas only a few short weeks ago?

"B.J.?"

She glanced toward her uncle, who sat watching her from the other side of the plane. "Yes?"

"Is that something you want your mother to see you wearing before you have a chance to explain what you've been up to?"

She didn't know what he meant at first. Following

the direction of his nod, she glanced down at her hands. She flushed when she realized she had been pensively spinning the gold band on her left ring finger.

How could she have forgotten Daniel's ring? Or the diamond bracelet on her right wrist? She stared at them, feeling her own identity slipping away again, leaving her confused about who exactly she had become.

"I—it's a long story," she said, her right hand closing over the ring to hide it from her uncle's view—and her own, as well.

"I figured it would be. We've got some time, if you want to talk."

How could she possibly explain how she had gotten so thoroughly swept up in Daniel's crazy charade that she was now having trouble remembering which parts had been real and which only make-believe?

Instead she asked, "What did you find out about Daniel Andreas?"

"Not much," Ryan admitted. "There's very little documentation about him for the past ten years."

"Is there any chance he's a federal agent?"

"Maybe. If so, he works undercover."

"But he could just be a con man."

"That's another possibility."

"Can you find out?"

"I still have a few strings to pull with the feds. But if he is undercover, neither he nor his superiors will appreciate us asking questions about him. And if they're looking for him, they're going to want to know what we know about him."

Which could lead someone straight to his aunt, whom he worried so much about protecting, B.J. thought, chewing on her lower lip.

She lifted her eyes to meet her uncle's. "Don't do anything yet," she said. "And I would appreciate it if you didn't mention this," she added, sliding the ring off her finger.

"If that's what you want."

"Thank you."

Her hand felt oddly bare when she slipped the ring into her wallet for safety. Only then did she notice that the snapshot of Daniel that she had carried in her wallet was missing. He must have taken it when he'd retrieved her things.

He hadn't even left her a photograph of himself, she thought with a clench in her heart. She knew he hadn't intended to leave his mother's ring with her.

It was only because so much had been going on around them that both of them had forgotten that ring. Maybe it had been wishful thinking on her part, she thought with a slight wince, but Daniel had more likely simply forgotten to take it back from her.

That was an oversight she intended to correct as soon as possible.

Chapter Fourteen

Maybe she was still jumpy from being spirited away to a luxury resort, stranded overnight on an island, locked in a storage closet and made love to by a dashing con man. Perhaps that explained why, almost two weeks after her return to Dallas, B.J. nearly jumped out of her shoes when someone knocked on the door of her apartment.

It was Saturday afternoon and she wasn't expecting anyone. She stuffed the gold band she had been holding into one pocket of her jeans and moved across the living room to check the peephole in her front door.

She didn't know who she had been expecting to

see—at least, not that she would admit—but she didn't know if she was more pleased or dismayed to see her mother's face in the distorted view of the peephole.

"Mom," she said, opening the door with a determinedly bright smile. "What are you doing here?"

"I suppose I should have called." Layla Walker Samples stepped over the threshold. "But I had a feeling you would be here."

Knowing her mother's pleasantly casual expression was as deceptive as her own smile, B.J. kissed the offered soft cheek and waved a hand toward the sofa. "Sit down. What can I get for you? Tea? Coffee? As you can see, I've been drinking a soda."

"Nothing right now, thank you. Sit next to me a moment, Brittany."

Her mother was the only person who had been allowed to call her that since B.J. announced on her sixteenth birthday that she preferred to use her initials. B.J. settled warily on one end of the couch, wondering what was coming next.

Layla reached out to take her hands. "When are you going to tell me what happened to you while you were away? I know it's still haunting you. You haven't been yourself since you got back."

Not herself. That was exactly the way B.J. had felt since she'd returned.

"You've been so distracted. You've lost weight— and you didn't have any to lose. I don't think I've seen you smile—not *really* smile—since you came home."

The obviously unsuccessful attempt at a smile that

B.J. had been wearing faded. Why bother when there was no fooling her mother?

"I know you were looking for Daniel Castillo," Layla continued. "Molly told me she asked you to find him to invite him to the big surprise party she's planning for Jared and Cassie. Did you find him?"

"I didn't exactly find Daniel Castillo."

"Is that why you've been upset? Because you feel like you failed in your assignment? You know Tony and Ryan and Joe will teach you more about being an investigator, if that's still what you're determined to do."

"I found Daniel, Mom."

Layla frowned in confusion. "But you said—"

"I said I didn't find Daniel Castillo. He uses the name Andreas now."

"I see. So you did find him. You talked to him."

"Yes."

"What's he like now? I remember him very well, you know. Of all the boys Jared and Cassie took in, I worried most about him. He was so angry. So defiant. Not that I blamed him, poor thing, after he lost his mother in such a terrible way. But I was concerned that you were so drawn to him. I knew you had a crush on him, of course."

"And you made sure I didn't spend much time alone with him."

"That's true," Layla admitted. "I figured you were a good influence on him—but I couldn't help worrying that he would be a bad influence on *you*."

Because that seemed so ironic in light of all that

happened after she found Daniel in Missouri, B.J. moistened her lips and stared at her hands.

"What's he like now?"

How was she to answer that? "Different," she said finally. "A little hard to describe."

"Did he turn out well? Is he a good man?"

Again B.J. was hard-pressed to answer. She settled for the reply that felt right to her. "He's a good man."

"Is he married?"

The gold band felt heavy in her pocket. "No."

"Is he coming to the party in October?"

"I don't think so."

"Molly will be disappointed."

"I know." B.J. reached for the half-empty glass of soda sitting on a coaster on the coffee table. She needed something to do to keep her hands occupied and to give her an excuse not to look into her mother's eyes as she evaded questions she wasn't yet prepared to answer.

Layla sighed lightly. "I tried to warn Molly not to get her hopes too high. All those troubled boys—there's no way for her to know what they've been up to since she saw them last. Some of them could very well have gone into lives of crime, for all we know."

B.J. choked on a sip of soda. She hastily set her glass on the table.

"Honey? Are you okay?"

"I'm fine, Mom. Thanks," she managed to reply.

"Anyway, I couldn't say much to Molly. Because after all, I didn't listen when people tried to discourage me from looking for my siblings all those years ago.

Since we were separated so young and raised in different foster homes and adoptive families, there was no
telling how everyone ended up. But I had to follow my
heart—and look how much joy my family has brought
to my life during the past twenty-five years."

B.J. had heard the story dozens of times, of course.
Layla and her six siblings had been split up after their
mother died when Jared, the eldest, was only eleven and
Lindsey not even a year old. Just over twenty-five years
ago, B.J.'s aunt Michelle had hired private investigator
Tony D'Alessandro to locate her biological siblings.
Layla, who had already been searching, was the first to
be found.

Eventually they had all been reunited, except for a
brother who had died in his late teens, leaving behind
a daughter. That daughter, Brynn, was now another be-
loved member of the extensive Walker family—as well
as the equally numerous D'Alessandro clan, since she
had married Tony's younger brother Joe.

Layla shook her head. "Molly's bound and determined to find out for herself what became of all those
foster boys she grew up with, and I'm certainly not
going to discourage her. Are you sure there's no chance
Daniel will come to the party?"

"I don't know. But I really doubt it."

"Is that why you've been so unhappy since you came
home? Because you feel like you let Molly down?"

B.J. should have known her mother wouldn't be de-
terred for long from trying to find out what was both-
ering her. "I'm fine, Mom. Really."

"Another life crisis?" Layla asked in resignation. "Have you decided private investigation isn't the career you want either?"

"I'm just...trying to make some difficult decisions." It wasn't that she didn't intend ever to tell her mother what had happened with Daniel; it was just that she wanted to do so after she herself knew how the story ended.

There was no need to worry Layla unnecessarily— and she *would* worry if she knew her daughter was tempted to pursue a man who might be a criminal. A man who had given no indication he even wanted to be found again.

Layla searched her face. "You aren't ready to talk about those decisions?"

"Not yet."

Her mother sighed and patted her knee. "You were always one who had to work everything out in your own mind before you turned to anyone else for advice. Just know that I'm here whenever you're ready to talk, all right?"

"I do know, Mom." She felt very blessed to realize that she had that constant, unwavering support base. It was a safety net that had been denied Daniel at much too young an age.

Layla rose to her feet, patting her thick hair, which was now more gray than brown. "I have an appointment at my beauty salon this afternoon, so I'll leave you to brood in peace. Call if you need me, okay?"

"I will."

"And eat something. You're too thin."

B.J. smiled. "I'll order a pizza."

Layla sighed heavily. "At least order veggies on it."

"It's a deal."

They hugged goodbye at the door. "Follow your heart, B.J.—it won't lead you wrong," Layla said as she stepped outside.

Follow your heart. The words seemed to echo in the apartment after B.J. closed the door.

It was not particularly deep or original advice, but it was an adage Layla had adhered to faithfully in her own lifetime. From marrying her college sweetheart to finding her long-lost siblings, Layla had followed her heart into a comfortable, happy maturity. If she had any regrets about any of the decisions she had made along the way, no one would ever guess for her almost always cheerful demeanor.

Follow your heart.

She pulled Daniel's ring from her jeans pocket and rubbed one fingertip across its smooth surface. On an impulse, she slid it onto her left ring finger, marveling as always at how perfectly it fit her.

Daniel would be wanting this back, she told herself. Of course, she could give it to his aunt, but she really wanted to hand it to him in person.

He still owed her a debt—and it was time for her to collect.

The tea was brewed strong enough to be more bitter than soothing, but B.J. drank it with a smile. "This is delicious."

Maria Sanchez smiled back at her. "It's nice to have company. Especially a friend of Daniel's."

"I'm trying to find him again," B.J. confessed. "I hoped you could give me a new lead."

"Daniel doesn't stay in one place for very long at a time," Maria said regretfully. "And he doesn't visit me often enough. The boy needs a permanent home."

"Do you know where he is now, Mrs. Sanchez?"

The old woman eyed her with still-shrewd dark eyes. "You want to invite him to another party?"

"No. I have something that belongs to him and I would like to return it personally." B.J. held out her hand, revealing the gold band resting on her palm.

Maria stared at the band. "My sister's ring."

"Yes."

"Where did you get it? Daniel never lets it out of his sight."

"He…let me borrow it. Now I need to give it back."

Setting down her teacup, Maria studied her so intently that B.J. almost squirmed in her seat. "You know about Daniel's mother."

B.J. nodded. "I know she was killed when a couple of junkies broke into her home to rob her."

"She was trying to raise her son alone after Daniel's father was killed in a bar fight. Anita had little formal education and she had some health problems that she never took the time to address properly. She didn't have much money, and the housing complex where she was forced to live was poorly maintained and overrun by drug dealers. The place was torn down years ago.

"Anyway, my sister planned to move as soon as she could, but she was killed before she could get away. Daniel found her when he came home from school."

"It must have been a nightmare for him." And even that, B.J. knew, was an understatement.

"The killers took an old television set, a pair of gold earrings that Daniel's father had given my sister and ten dollars in cash," Maria said bitterly. "They probably would have taken the wedding band she always wore, but it was very tight on her finger and they must have been in a hurry to get away."

B.J.'s hand tightened spasmodically around the ring that meant so much to Daniel.

"I wanted to take Daniel, but I was battling breast cancer at the time," Maria added. "There was no one else. He was so angry and rebellious that I worried about him getting into serious trouble. He was placed in two foster homes that didn't work out for him before he was sent to your uncle's ranch."

"My uncle has a special bond with angry teenage boys," B.J. said. "Probably because he was one himself."

"I saw the difference in Daniel as soon as he came home to me when I was able to care for him. He was still very quiet but respectful and focused on his studies. He lived with me until he completed high school and he has been taking care of me ever since."

"And do you know what he's been doing during those years?" B.J. asked quietly.

"He tells me he works with computers. I think he

tells me this so I won't worry about him," Maria added, once again displaying the astuteness that must have made it difficult for Daniel to deceive her.

"Do you know how to reach him now?"

"I have his cell phone number for emergency use only. He calls me from it twice a week."

B.J. gazed steadily at the older woman. "I know it's asking a lot, but will you give me that number?"

She could use the number to trace where the calls had come from, perhaps. After all, she had a few strings to pull, if necessary, she told herself, picturing her uncle Ryan's face.

Maria considered her question for a moment and then she smiled. "When you came to me last time telling me about the party, I helped you partly because I thought it would be nice for Daniel to visit the ranch again and thank the people who had been so good to him."

B.J. was curious about her wording. "What was the other reason?"

"I recognized you from a photograph Daniel keeps in his possession. It's almost as precious to him, I think, as his mother's ring."

B.J. was stunned. "A—a photograph? Of me?"

Maria nodded her gray head. "You are a young girl, standing next to Daniel. There are horses in the background, and you are smiling at him. Even in that old photograph, I could see that you were very fond of him."

B.J. actually remembered Cassie taking that snapshot during a Fourth of July party at the ranch. Cassie had taken dozens of pictures that day, and B.J. had seen them all. She hadn't realized Daniel had carried one of them with him when he left.

"My Daniel is a good man, B.J., but he is too much alone. He needs a home. A family. I sent you to him before because I think he has always cared about you. And from the way you have spoken of him today, I think you care about him, too."

B.J. didn't bother to deny it. "Yes. Very much."

Maria smiled. "Then go find him. And you may tell him I sent you to him."

Sighing, B.J. looked at the ring again. "It isn't going to be easy. Daniel has his emotions locked away so tightly, I'm not sure he knows how to let them out now."

"Then teach him. The things that matter most in life aren't the ones that come most easily, B.J."

Gazing into the eyes of the woman whose wisdom had come through years of hard experience, B.J. was amazed that Maria could still sound so hopeful and optimistic. She had a feeling that Maria would get along very well with her mother.

Daniel's steps dragged as he trudged through an alley toward the ratty Chicago apartment building in which he had lived for the past two and a half weeks. The heavy biker boots contributed in part to his sluggish movements, but not as much as the weariness that permeated all the way through to his bones.

His face itched. He scratched absently at the thick

stubble that darkened his cheeks and chin. His hair felt long against the back of his neck and heavy with the gel he'd applied liberally to it. The stained T-shirt and ragged jeans he wore didn't fit very well and they weren't overly comfortable.

He couldn't help thinking of the impeccably tailored suits and casual clothing made of the finest fabrics that he'd worn at the resort last month. Few people who had seen him then would recognize him now as the same man. Which was exactly the point, of course.

As he turned a corner into a second alley, this one even darker and smellier than the last, he tried to push thoughts of the resort to the back of his mind. There were some memories that were just too painful to dwell on. That half hour when he hadn't known where B.J. was or whether she was safe was one of those memories.

Had she had any idea of how worried he had been? How frantically he had searched for her as soon as he had managed to slip out of Drake's office during the pandemonium of the raid? How relieved he had been when he'd heard she was safe?

Maybe she'd thought he hadn't cared. After all, he'd cut out immediately, hadn't even tried to contact her to tell her personally how sorry he was that Drake had dared to threaten her.

Could she possibly know that she hadn't been out of his thoughts for more than a few minutes at a time since he'd left her, even when he had done his best to think of *anything* else?

I just want you to know I'm in love with you.

He doubted that she would say those words so trust-ingly to him now, a month after he'd abandoned her at the resort. After she had returned to the family that had no trouble showing her just how much she meant to them. The family who would protect her from danger rather than leading her into it.

It hadn't really been love, he told himself, as he did every time he heard those words in his memory. Not on her part, anyway. As for himself…

He wasn't afraid of much. But even the thought of letting himself love someone—B.J., specifically—made him break out into a cold sweat.

He winced as he reached the end of the alley. His lower back ached from a well-placed kick in the kid-neys earlier that day. He'd let himself be blindsided—and he hadn't even been thinking about B.J. at the time.

Maybe he was getting too old for the life he'd been leading. He sure felt like it now.

A rustle of sound from his left was the only warning he had before someone slammed into him from behind.

Daniel staggered and almost went down, but he re-gained his footing at the last moment. He started to turn to fight, but someone else caught him from the other side, slamming a fist into his jaw with enough force that Daniel saw stars for a moment.

Another fist hit him in the stomach. Doubling over, he drew a deep, painfully ragged breath and came up fighting, using his fists and heavy boots to put up a de-fense against the two thugs who had jumped him.

Daniel saw the gleam of a knife just in time to throw himself to one side, avoiding the wild slash. He used his momentum to slam his booted foot into the guy's shin. The attacker yelped and reeled backward. Unfortunately, he didn't drop the knife.

Keeping one eye on that blade, Daniel slammed his elbow into the solar plexus of the other assailant, following that with a hard kick to the side of the knee. While that man hobbled and cursed, Daniel kicked upward toward the arm of the man holding the knife, who dodged and thrust wildly in response.

Daniel felt the slash of pain on his forearm, the hot rush of blood, but he stayed focused on the fight. He didn't allow himself to be distracted even when he heard a yell and the sound of running feet headed their way.

"It's a girl," the guy with the knife sneered before swinging at Daniel again. "Take care of her, Mike."

Cursing beneath his breath, Daniel dodged and kicked out again. Great. Some woman was trying to be a hero, and now he was going to have to protect her, too, when he had his hands full fighting off the two men who had caught him so off guard—and this time because he *had* been thinking about B.J.

The knife wielder thrust with a sudden, forceful move. Daniel caught the man's wrist from below in his left hand, then brought the outside of his right fist down solidly on top of the guy's arm. There was a satisfying crack of bone and a howl of pain.

Daniel finished the guy off with a hard kick to the kneecap, eliciting another rather high-pitched shriek, and then he threw him aside. Scooping up the knife, he turned to help whoever had foolishly run to his rescue.

He lifted his eyebrows in surprise when he saw a slender woman in blue jeans and a bright pink T-shirt bent over the man who lay on his stomach beneath her, his arm twisted behind his back, his neck immobilized beneath her sneakered right foot.

Even as Daniel watched, she exerted pressure on the guy's neck and arm at the same time, causing him to grunt and squirm. "You're breaking my freakin' arm!" he groaned, sounding both alarmed and chagrined.

"I'm going to break your freakin' neck if you move again," the woman advised him.

Recognition slammed through Daniel with the force of another blow. "B.J."

She glanced at him without releasing her hold on the man she held down. "Got something to tie him up with?"

Still stunned, he automatically removed his leather belt and strapped the man's wrists tightly behind his back. The other man was still nursing his injured arm, his leg twisted ominously beneath him.

"You broke my arm," he said accusingly when Daniel reached for him. His voice was thickened by the blood that ran from his nose. "And you've done something to my knee."

"Consider yourself lucky I didn't fillet you with your own knife." A bit over the top, maybe, but he couldn't let B.J. sound tougher than he did.

Confident that both his assailants were immobilized,

he whipped his cell phone out of his pocket and made a quick call.

He waited only until he heard sirens very close by before turning to B.J., who had been standing quietly nearby, keeping a watchful eye on the sullen men they had subdued. "Let's get out of here."

She lifted her eyebrows. "Before the police arrive?"

"They'll be here in less than a minute. These two aren't in any shape to get away before that."

"But don't we need to—"

He settled the argument by the simple measure of taking her arm and giving a slight tug. "Let's go."

It was hard to believe this was the same man she had been with less than a month earlier. B.J. studied Daniel appraisingly. At the resort he had been tailored, groomed, styled and immaculate. This man was un-shaven, grubby, disheveled and dripping blood on the dirty carpet of the dingy apartment to which he had led her.

The only thing the two images had in common was that they both looked dangerous. Yet she was no more afraid of this one than she had been of the other.

"You should probably do something about that arm," she advised him, keeping all emotion out of her voice—which wasn't easy. "You're bleeding all over your new tattoos."

He glanced down at his bloody ink-embellished arm and scowled. "They're fake."

"I figured. But the blood is real."

"It'll keep. What are you doing here?"

She looked at her slightly raw right fist. She'd known better than to use her knuckles in a fight. "Saving your butt again, apparently."

That made his scowl deepen. "I didn't need your help."

"Against two men and a knife? The odds weren't exactly in your favor."

"They were amateurs. I could have handled them."

"Maybe. But I wasn't going to stand by and watch."

"You shouldn't have been there at all. How the hell did you find me again?"

She sighed and shook her head. "I'm sorry, Daniel, but I can't talk to you while you're standing there bleeding. Since I don't suppose you'd be willing to see a doctor, is there any chance you have a first-aid kit?"

He hesitated a minute, then turned on one heel and disappeared into the bathroom. B.J. took a minute to look around the apartment. It was only one room, with a kitchenette against one wall and a sitting room/sleeping room taking up the rest of the space. There was no dining area; she supposed Daniel ate off the rickety coffee table that sat in front of a tattered sleeper sofa.

All in all, it was a far cry from the luxury suite in which they had stayed at Drake's resort.

Looking just like a man one would expect to find in a place like this, Daniel returned then, carrying a small plastic case. He tossed it on the coffee table.

"Just slap a bandage on it, if you must," he said grudgingly. "Then I want some answers."

"Sit down. I'm getting a washcloth. I'm not putting a bandage on a dirty wound."

His sigh was a gusty, impatient exhale. Ignoring him, she walked into the bathroom, pulled a threadbare white washcloth from a cabinet and held it under the faucet. Carrying the dripping cloth, a matching towel and a bar of soap back into the other room, she noted that he sat on the couch, as she had suggested.

His face was just a bit pale beneath the beard and the grime. Apparently he was feeling the injury more than he allowed himself to let on. Stubborn man.

Perching beside him, she cleaned the wound as best as she could with soap and alcohol pads—smearing a tattoo of a coiled rattlesnake in the process. Keeping her opinion of that professional-looking artwork to herself, she focused on applying antibiotic ointment to the slice in his bicep, then covering it carefully with gauze and tape.

Daniel remained still during the process, his expression unrevealing. If she was hurting him, she couldn't tell. If he was affected in any way by her touch, she couldn't detect that either.

She hoped her own face was equally inscrutable. Because sitting next to him, treating the ugly wound on his arm, touching him was definitely affecting *her*.

Chapter Fifteen

Daniel wasn't sure if the burning in his arm was due more to his injury or the feel of B.J.'s hands on his skin. It was something he had never thought he would feel again, and his reaction was so intense it bordered right on the edge of pain.

He still couldn't believe she was here. Couldn't believe she had tracked him down again. Was he so easy to find? If so, it was definitely time for him to get into a new line of work.

"There," she said, eyeing her handiwork in satisfaction. "Maybe your arm won't fall off now."

"That's comforting."

Without replying, she stuffed the first-aid supplies

back in the case and snapped it shut. "You'll probably want to take alcohol to the rest of that tattoo. Looks kind of silly to have half a snake on your arm."

He suddenly felt rather foolish in his tough street disguise. Even when she had been dressed in clothes that were not her own, pretending to be someone she wasn't, B.J. was completely herself. Daniel didn't know who the hell he was these days.

He glanced sideways at her face, noting that her hair was still mussed from the fight, she wore little if any makeup and there was a smudge on her nose. She was every bit as beautiful to him then as she had ever been in her expensive resort clothes.

So much for a whole month of trying to get over her.

"Damn it, B.J. why are you here?" Even he heard the deep weariness in his voice.

She dropped the defensiveness, her expression going somber. "I needed to return something to you."

She reached into her pocket and then held out her left hand. Daniel stared at the gold band on her palm.

Rather than taking it from her, he clasped his hands between his knees. Ever since he'd left the resort, he had been aware of the ring's absence. After all, he had worn it around his neck for more than a dozen years. But whenever he'd thought of the ring during the past month, he hadn't pictured it hanging on a chain around his neck. He had seen it on B.J.'s delicate hand.

That thought drew his eyes to her nervously clenched right hand, with its reddened knuckles. Evidence of the way she had thrown herself into a fight between him and two other men, one of whom had wielded a knife.

Maybe not so delicate, after all, he thought with a humorless twitch at the corner of his mouth. But infinitely precious to him.

"When did you learn martial arts?"

His incongruous question seemed to take her aback. She lowered the hand that was holding his ring and eyed him quizzically. "I dated a tae kwon do instructor in college. I got as high as brown belt before we broke up."

"Why didn't you mention it at the resort?"

"It never came up."

"You didn't try to use it when Drake's man shoved you into a closet?" He had heard from Greg, through Ingrid, where B.J. had been stashed.

That brought her chin up, her eyes snapping indignantly. "I thought he was the person you had sent. And I was...thinking about something else."

Daniel turned sideways on the couch and covered her hands with his, the gold ring folded out of sight in her palm. "B.J., why did you come here? You could have sent the ring to my aunt."

She drew a deep breath. "You said you owed me a favor. You told me to name my price. I'm here to collect."

Daniel swallowed hard. He had a feeling this debt was going to be higher than he had expected to pay.

B.J. watched the wariness cross Daniel's face. His fingers tightened momentarily around hers. "What is it you want?" he asked somewhat roughly.

Keeping her gaze steady on his, she reminded herself of the way he had looked when he had recognized her in that alley. For one brief, unguarded moment, she had seen true emotion in his eyes—and she hoped desperately that she hadn't misread him.

"I'll tell you that in a minute. First, I want to ask you something."

"What?"

"Why did those men attack you?"

He wasn't expecting that. "I think it was retribution. I sort of messed up a deal they were putting together," he said after a moment.

"A drug deal?"

He fell back on a particularly irritating habit he had developed the last time they'd been together. He didn't answer.

She sighed. "I just wanted to see if you would be honest with me this time. I know you're a fed. I know you work undercover. I know you were setting Drake up for the bust last month and that he thought you were buying into his drug cartel with your 'rich wife's' money."

Daniel's eyes were narrowed now, his mouth set in a display of irritation. "Anything else you want to tell me about myself?" he asked too politely, releasing her hands and crossing his arms over his chest in a gesture that she interpreted as self-protective.

"Why didn't you tell me what you are before? Why did you lead me to believe you were a con man?"

"I didn't say that. You did," he reminded her.

"Yet you didn't correct me. Why?"

"I thought you would be safer if you didn't know everything."

"That's not the reason. Not entirely, anyway."

He glared at her, his temper mounting visibly. "I didn't want you romanticizing what I do. I'm no movie hero. I chose this career because the money's pretty good, I get bored easily in more routine jobs and I'm sort of a danger junkie. Not for any more noble reason."

"Okay, I get the picture. You're a tough-guy cop."

His scowl only deepened. "I just didn't want you to confuse the boy I was with the man I am now."

"Because, of course, I'm too stupid to know the difference." This time she was the one who spoke with exaggerated civility.

He grunted impatiently. "I didn't say that."

"It was sort of a given from the way you said it."

"Look, I know you're not stupid. It's just—"

"You knew I had a big crush on you when we were kids."

"Maybe. And then you—"

"I told you I was in love with you at the resort."

His throat worked with a hard swallow. "Yeah. That, too."

"And you thought I had confused the two of you. Boy and man, I mean."

"Well—"

She couldn't help smiling at him, though she knew it was shaky. "I know you're not the same person you were thirteen years ago, Daniel. Neither am I. We've both had full lives since we parted back then. But there's still a connection between us, I think."

Maybe the direction the conversation was veering into worried him. He abruptly changed the subject. "How *did* you find me this time? And how did you learn what I do? Your uncles?"

"I found you because I talked to your aunt again. Even though she doesn't know exactly what to do, she has her suspicions. She was able to give me enough information to track you."

"Damn it."

"If it makes you feel any better, no one else has ever contacted her about you," she told him. "I really like her, Daniel. She's a very shrewd woman."

He merely scowled.

"As for what you do—well, I figured that out for myself. It took me a while and a little digging, but mostly I just knew you had to be working on the right side of the law. The Daniel I knew wouldn't work with drug dealers when drugs had already cost him so much."

He looked broodingly at her. "I told you not to romanticize me."

"I can't help it, a little," she murmured. "I admire what you do—no matter what reasons you claim might motivate you. I appreciate how good you've been to your aunt. And I'm impressed by the way you've gotten to where you are pretty much on your own."

He started to speak, but she didn't give him a chance.

"That doesn't mean I think you're perfect," she told him firmly. "You can still be a jerk sometimes. Bossy and arrogant. Leaving me that way at the resort was really rotten of you. So was letting me wonder for so long whether you were as bad as Drake. Making decisions for me based on your assumption that I'm too dumb to make them for myself. That *really* makes me mad."

"I never said you were dumb." He was beginning to sound defensive now.

"And I don't like the way you refuse to talk to me about what you're thinking and feeling, leaving me to try to guess and risk making a fool of myself. I don't like it when you—"

"So your point is?" he interrupted.

"My point is, I know exactly who you are. The man. The cop. The jerk."

"Would you quit calling me that?"

Her mouth twitched. "Starting to bug you?"

She was immeasurably relieved to see what might have been a mere hint of answering humor in his dark eyes. "Yeah."

"So maybe I can be a little jerky sometimes myself."

"Maybe so." Growing somber again, he looked down. "I want you to know that I'm not brushing off your feelings. You have to know you're very special to me, too. But—"

"But?" she prodded when he fell silent.

"You deserve better," he said in a rush. "You deserve someone who knows how to build a real home. A real family. Someone who isn't prone to dragging you into danger."

"Daniel—"

This time he was the one determined to have his say. "I haven't lived in the same place for more than a few months since I left my aunt's house when I was eighteen. I've never had what you would call a serious relationship. I change my identity so often, I don't even know who I am half the time. I could just as easily have been using a fake name as my own when you found me in Missouri. I've been answering to Jonas Lopez for the past three weeks."

She lifted her right hand to his beard-shadowed face. "I know."

"Don't look at me like that," he said roughly.

"I'm sorry. I don't seem to have any control over the way I look at you."

"You aren't listening to a word I say, are you?"

"I'm listening to *every* word you say," she countered quietly. "And it breaks my heart that you think so little of yourself."

He started to rebut that, but she slid her hand from his cheek to cover his mouth. "We've never really talked about that day beside the pond years ago. Maybe we should talk about it now."

It didn't surprise her that he was shaking his head even before she finished the sentence.

"You told me that day that you blamed yourself for not protecting your mother," she continued quickly, before he could turn away. "You thought you should have been able to somehow prevent what happened to her. You said you were afraid to care about anyone else because you were afraid something bad would happen to them."

His face was hot, his eyes haunted as she recounted that conversation he must have found so painful then. So mortifying now. "I was a kid and still hurting over finding her. I said things to you that I hadn't been able to say to anyone else."

"I know. And I'm really not confusing you again with that troubled boy, Daniel. But I want to make sure *you* aren't confusing the past and present either. That you aren't still afraid to take the risk of loving anyone because of that misguided guilt over your mother's death. You worry about your aunt being associated with you and hardly ever visit her. As for me—I don't need to be protected. Nothing is going to happen to me for loving you."

"How can you say that after everything that has happened to you because of me?" he said through clenched teeth, catching her right hand and holding it so tightly she almost winced. He turned her hand palm down to reveal her reddened knuckles. "What about this?"

Glancing down at the bruised skin, she wrinkled her nose. "My fault. I knew better than to punch with my knuckles."

"It wasn't your fault. *Nothing* has been your fault. It's all been because of me."

"I have to admit I've never been bored around you," she said.

"This isn't a joke, B.J. You could have been hurt. Or—"

"But I wasn't," she said, turning her hand to grip his. "Because I can take care of myself."

"I couldn't take it if anything happened to you." His voice sounded strained, as if he were forcing the words out through a tight throat.

Hope knotted inside her own throat, threatening to choke her. "Maybe this is a good time for me to collect on that debt."

He pushed an unsteady hand through his overlong hair. "What do you want?"

"One completely honest answer," she whispered.

Looking as though he would rather she had demanded a kidney, he pushed away from her and rose to his feet. "I'm not playing games with you."

Staying where she was, she gazed up at him. "Good. I'm very serious. You said you owed me—and that's all I want from you. Just one answer."

He sighed. "Fine. Get it over with."

Not very encouraging, she thought, studying his set shoulders and braced feet. Maybe he thought she would lose her nerve if he was forbidding enough.

He should have known her better.

Clinging to the memory of the expression in his eyes when he had said he couldn't take it if she were hurt, she drew a deep breath and blurted, "Do you love me?"

She thought at first that he wasn't going to answer, despite his agreement. He kept his back half-turned to her when he finally said, "Yes."

No elaboration. No qualification. And no encouragement, she couldn't help noting. He had given her exactly what she'd asked for and nothing more.

Still, it gave her more reason to hope....

"Will you give us a chance?"

"It wouldn't work," he said, his voice so low she had to strain to hear him. "I'm no good at that sort of thing. I travel too much. And I know how hard it is to be married to someone in my line of work, never knowing from one day to the next whether you're going to be a widow."

"That would be difficult for me," she admitted. "But I could learn to deal with it if you're committed to your job. I would never ask you to leave it for my sake."

"It's all I know how to do. I'm not fooling myself that I make that big a difference in a world where three more scumbags pop up whenever we put one behind bars. But at least I can say I tried to make things a little better, one bust at a time."

"Like Uncle Jared and his foster boys—helping a few out of the many who are in trouble. I hope you can forgive me for saying you were more like Judson Drake than Jared Walker. That was a low blow—and so very wrong."

He shook his head forcefully. "I'll never be the man Jared is. Some of the things I've done…"

"Daniel." She rose then, moving to face him fully. "Didn't you listen to any of our family history while you were with us? When Jared's siblings finally located him, he was in jail. He was a drifter who had been arrested for an armed robbery he didn't commit, leaving his young son alone on the streets until Cassie found him and helped him clear Jared's name.

"Despite the way the rest of the family pretty much idolizes him, Jared is the first to deny that he's anyone's hero. He calls himself a simple cowboy with a knack for taming horses and teenage boys. A man with flaws and emotional baggage from being raised by an alcoholic father and a mother who died much too young— not to mention spending the rest of his youth in foster homes and his early adulthood trying to find a place for himself. Now he's chosen to try to make a difference in the world, a little at a time. Don't tell me you aren't like him, Daniel. I know better."

He looked stunned, though he was still shaking his head. "Don't—"

"I'm not confusing you with him. I haven't been looking specifically for a man like Jared, though I've always admired him, so it isn't surprising I would fall for someone who reminds me of him in some ways. I'm in love with *you,* Daniel Andreas or Castillo or Lopez or Smith— whatever you call yourself, whatever you do for a living. And I won't stop loving you even if you send me away again. I'll just spend the rest of my life missing you."

"You deserve better."

"You're right. I do," she replied steadily. "And you deserve better than what you've had, too. You deserve a real home. Someone who loves you for exactly who you are rather than the roles you've played for so long. A chance to forgive yourself for things you had no control over. So what are you going to do about it?"

He heaved a long, weary-sounding sigh that might have signaled surrender. "How do you feel about answering to Mrs. Andreas again? I'd rather not go back to Castillo, since I left that part of my life behind a long time ago."

She should have been expecting something like that, considering that Daniel had a habit of giving her no warning before doing something that knocked the breath completely out of her. After taking a moment to steady herself, she replied, "I could get used to it."

"Because if you prefer Smith…"

She shook her head and gave him a tremulous smile. "Andreas is fine."

His tone turned suddenly fierce. "Be sure," he said. "Because I'm sure as hell not going to apologize this time, either, if you change your mind later."

Her smile deepened at the reminder of the first time he had made love to her. "I won't change my mind. And I won't need an apology, because I have no doubt that we can make this work. I love you, Daniel."

She saw the courage it took for him to look her in the eyes and reply, "I love you, too. God help you."

And then he held out his arms to her.

They took their time from that point. Daniel insisted on shaving and showering, getting rid of the last signs of the unkempt "Jonas Lopez." Insisting that he needed help showering—just to make sure he didn't reopen the slice in his arm—B.J. joined him.

The hot water didn't last long, but the heat they generated between them more than made up for it.

Afterward they made love on the sleeper sofa, barely taking time to throw aside the cushions and unfold the bed first. Daniel seemed genuinely embarrassed at first by the grubbiness of the apartment, but she convinced him rather quickly that she didn't care where they were as long as they were together.

Together, they proved almost immediately that the surroundings didn't matter. Whether in a luxury suite or on a picnic table or between the sheets of a tattered bed, they found paradise whenever they were together. And paradise was even sweeter this time because they both knew it wouldn't be the last time they visited there.

B.J. was still wondering whether she would ever breathe normally again when Daniel spoke, his voice still a bit hoarse. "About that tae kwon do instructor…"

She was surprised into a giggle. "What about him?"

"Could he have kicked my ass?"

Daniel would have pounded Tommy into the ground, but B.J. saw no point in inflating his ego any more than she already had for one day. Still smiling, she murmured, "Let's just say I've always had a thing for tough guys."

"Does that mean…?"

She rolled over onto his chest, propping her chin on her hands. "Anyone ever tell you that you've got the prettiest eyes?"

"You're trying to change the subject."

"Yes. But they *are* pretty."

Daniel sighed and shook his head, silently acknowledging that she wouldn't answer any more questions about the ex-boyfriend.

"So—think I can find a job in Dallas? Maybe the police department is hiring."

She was a bit surprised by the new topic, but she answered easily enough. "I'm sure one of my uncles can pull a few strings with the Dallas PD—but are you sure that's what you want to do? Give up what you're doing now to settle into one place?"

He shrugged, but she knew he wasn't taking her question lightly. "Part of the reason I was so good at this job is because I had no real ties to anyone, no place I had to be, no one to worry about me if I suddenly disappeared. I made arrangements for Aunt Maria to be taken care of if anything happened to me, but I also made sure there was nothing else connecting her to me. Things are different now. As Drake pointed out, you've become my weakness."

She frowned, uncertain if that was a good thing.

"It isn't a criticism," he assured her, reading her expression. "It feels pretty good to know someone would care if I didn't make it home."

"You're underestimating the way your aunt feels about you. She loves you very much. And she would care deeply if you didn't make it home."

"Then that's another reason for me to settle down in one place and take a job that's a little more secure. I could see her. And being the wife of a cop isn't a picnic, but it's better than what I can offer you now."

"I'll take it," she said promptly. "Happily. But be sure, Daniel. I won't apologize if you change your mind later."

He flashed a grin in response to her quoting him. "I won't expect you to."

B.J. rested her head on his chest, contentment flooding through her. And then she suddenly groaned and lifted her head again. "Uh-oh. I think you're going to have to come up with one more cover story."

His eyebrows rose quizzically. "What?"

"Jared and Cassie aren't supposed to find out about the surprise party being planned for October. They don't know Molly sent me looking for you. Since I have no intention of waiting nearly four months to bring you back into the family, we've got to make up a story about how we ran into each other again completely by accident."

"How about we tell them that I kidnapped you and had my wicked way with you until you agreed to marry me?"

She grinned but shook her head. "They would never believe that."

He touched her cheek. "Then maybe we should tell them that I've been in love with you since I was sixteen and I finally had the good sense to do something about it."

"I like that," she murmured, shaken by the ring of truth in his deep voice. "Maybe we'll come up with a variation of it."

He caught the back of her neck in one hand and pulled her down for a long, deep kiss. Wrapping her arms around him, B.J. decided it didn't really matter what they told anyone else.

They had always been meant to be together. One way or another, they would have found each other again. This time it was forever.

* * * * *

Don't miss Gina Wilkins's next romance,
The Road to Reunion
available next month.

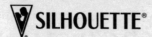

❤ SILHOUETTE®

1106/23b

SPECIAL EDITION™

HAILEY'S HERO
by Judy Duarte

Bayside Bachelors

A night of passion with Detective Nick Granger had left Hailey Conway pregnant and facing a dilemma: does she tell the man who had sworn he'd never be a father and a husband that she is carrying his baby?

THE CHRISTMAS FEAST
by Peggy Webb

Zany and carefree Jolie showed her family she was a responsible adult by cooking Christmas dinner—with the help of one surprise guest. Undercover agent Lance Estes was charmed by Jolie…and began heating things up in the kitchen!

THE FATHER FACTOR
by Lilian Darcy

A sizzling affair with Jared Starke, the hotshot big-city corporate lawyer, had led to an unexpected pregnancy for Shallis Duncan , but could she trust him enough to tell him—especially when he'd just received other news…?

▼ SILHOUETTE®
𝒮𝓊𝓅𝑒𝓇ROMANCE™

HOME FOR CHRISTMAS by Carrie Weaver
Suddenly a Parent

Most men have nine months to prepare to be a father. Not Beau Stanton. Still, he's determined to be a great dad to his new daughter. And that means the end to his days as a footloose bachelor and then he meets Nancy McGuire...

A DIFFERENT KIND OF MAN
by Suzanne Cox
Count on a Cop

Emalea LeBlanc and investigator Jackson Cooper start off at odds when Emalea wins Jackson's motorbike in a race. Emalea believes that Jackson is the type of man she needs to avoid. But is there more to Jackson than meets the eye?

NOT WITHOUT HER SON by Kay David
The Operatives

Julia Vandamme's nightmare began after she said 'I do.' Her only comfort is her sweet little boy, and she has stayed in her marriage just for him. Jonathan Cruz is her one chance for escape.

A MUM FOR MATTHEW by Roz Denny Fox
Single Father

Zeke Rossetti's busy life, caring for five-year-old Matthew and managing a demanding business, doesn't really allow for distractions. Grace Stafford is definitely a distraction. Grace might be the woman for him—but can she be a mum for Matthew?

On sale from 17th November 2006

Available at WHSmith, Tesco, ASDA, Borders, Eason, Sainsbury's and most bookshops

www.silhouette.co.uk

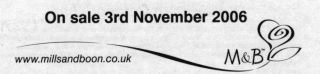

FREE

4 BOOKS AND A SURPRISE GIFT!

We would like to take this opportunity to thank you for reading this Silhouette® book by offering you the chance to take FOUR more specially selected titles from the Special Edition™ series absolutely FREE! We're also making this offer to introduce you to the benefits of the Mills & Boon® Reader Service™—

- ★ **FREE home delivery**
- ★ **FREE gifts and competitions**
- ★ **FREE monthly Newsletter**
- ★ **Books available before they're in the shops**
- ★ **Exclusive Reader Service offers**

Accepting these FREE books and gift places you under no obligation to buy; you may cancel at any time, even after receiving your free shipment. Simply complete your details below and return the entire page to the address below. You don't even need a stamp!

YES! Please send me 4 free Special Edition books and a surprise gift. I understand that unless you hear from me, I will receive 6 superb new titles every month for just £3.10 each, postage and packing free. I am under no obligation to purchase any books and may cancel my subscription at any time. The free books and gift will be mine to keep in any case.

E6ZEE

Ms/Mrs/Miss/Mr...Initials ....
                                                                    BLOCK CAPITALS PLEASE
Surname ....
Address ....

....

....Postcode ....

Send this whole page to:

The Reader Service, FREEPOST CN81, Croydon, CR9 3WZ